"Don't move," he cried. "I've got you."—*Page* 204.

HIS LUCKIEST YEAR

BY

FRANCIS J. FINN, S.J.

Author of "Percy Wynn," "Tom Playfair,"
"Harry Dee," etc.

New York, Cincinnati, Chicago

BENZIGER BROTHERS

CONTENTS

CHAPTER I

HIS LUCKIEST YEAR

A SEQUEL TO "LUCKY BOB"

CHAPTER I

Showing how Bob Ryan in trying to be kind is,, in effect, looking for trouble.

ON the last Saturday of September, as the bells of St. Xavier announced the morning hour of ten, a chubby youth, faultlessly dressed and looking the picture of joy and health, emerged from a house on Pioneer Street, Cincinnati, glanced up and down, and then turned briskly eastward. The boy carried under his right arm a rather large package. It looked as though the contents were oranges; and that they were oranges beyond all doubt any one with a sense of smell could have certainly attested.

It was a bright, crisp morning, with a touch of autumn in the air. It was good to be out on such a day. Certainly the rosy youth seemed to think so; for he threw out his chest and took several deep breaths, stepping forward briskly as he did so. Pioneer Street, apparently, was deserted. It is the easy custom of the school children residing on that

famous though short thoroughfare to lie abed late on Saturdays. The Saturday late sleep, in fact, has become a tradition. Ten o'clock on that particular day of the week is the hour of rising. The boy therefore—who, it should be said, was an alien on the street, having resided there only a few weeks— did not expect to meet or greet any of his new friends. But he was agreeably disappointed.

Miss Alice O'Shea, residing in the neat two-story frame house which faces and blocks Pike Street, casting a chance look out of her window as she was engaged in the completion of her simple Saturday-morning toilet—much simpler, of course, than on the days when school was held — caught sight of the ruddy stranger. Alice, aged eleven, good-natured almost to a fault, liked the new boy. He was good-natured, too. Had he not presented her with an apple a few days ago, apropos of nothing? Had he not always greeted her with a smile? When she got up her birthday party she had settled that among her guests Bob Ryan should be the Abou Ben Adhem of the list, and lead all the rest.

Some children there are who bask in smiles. They love the cheery face. Alice was just that sort of girl. There was nothing sentimental about this blue-eyed, fair-complexioned, and, under her mother's dextrous fingers, curly-haired girl. She was matter-of-fact, and loved the smile of welcome or of farewell as she loved the sunshine and the caressing airs of springtime. On perceiving the youth, therefore, advancing down the other side of the street, Alice gathered up her hair in one comprehensive sweep of her two hands, massed it into a ball, and with a hasty hairpin or two, with a resultant effect not altogether lovely, pinned it into stability; and taking a perfunctory glance into the mirror, rushed to the front door, darted out, and tripped across the street, just in time to catch her quarry as he was about to turn into Pike.

Alice's industry did not go unrewarded: the stalwart lad, who looked full sixteen, though he was not yet fourteen, turned an eye of welcome upon the gingham-gowned, barefooted apparition, and smiled beamingly.

"Good morning, Alice!" he exclaimed.

"Good morning, Bob Ryan," returned Alice with a smile little inferior to the boy's.

Alice allowed her gaze to wander from Bob's face to the bundle under his arm. Curiosity got the better of this lineal descendent of Mother Eve. She sniffed the air, and said, with a question mark in her intonation:

"Oranges?"

"Yes," returned Bob Ryan. "You know Albert Corcoran?"

"The eighth-grade boy who's down with typhoid?"

"Yes ; but he's not exactly down now. He's convalescent, you know."

"Oh, dear!" cried Alice, "do you think he'll die?"

"Dye what?" broke in a strange voice, "his whiskers? He ain't got any yet, and you'll be peroxidizing your hair a long time before he'll find it worth while buying a razor."

Alice turned a severe eye toward a window whence issued these words. Master Johnny O'Brien, their utterer, stood grinning there. It had never occurred to Johnny O'Brien, aged twelve, in the course of his natural life that any conversation held on Pioneer Street was confidential or not intended for his ears. He was always putting in his oar.

"You easy-dropper!" she flung out.

"I ain't," protested Johnny, appalled by the unaccustomed word, and wondering what it meant.

"You go on upstairs and wash your face," continued Alice. "This conversation is private — you hear?"

Bob chuckled. John looked contrite.

"I didn't intend to butt in," he protested.

"Well, you did," insisted Alice.

"John—you John," came a rich alto voice from above, "you come right up and get your neck washed, or not a step out of this house will you stir to-day."

At which dire threat John incontinently departed. Had he heard the conversation that followed, Bob Ryan might have been saved considerable trouble on that particular morning.

"I was saying," Bob resumed, "that Albert is convalescent, which means he's well but weak. All he needs is to get his strength again."

"That's what I thought," said Alice bravely. "But you're not going to his house, are you?"

"Of course I am."

"But don't you know, Bob, that he lives on EUen Street?"

"I've got his number, all right."

"Did you ever see an Ellen Street boy on Pioneer Street, Bob?"

Bob paused and knotted his fair brow.

"I can't say I have," he presently answered.

"There ain't been an Ellen Street boy or a Kilgour Street boy on Pioneer since last June," continued Alice. "And there ain't been a Pioneer Street boy on those streets since last June."

"Is that so?" asked Bob.

"No," continued the girl, giving her somewhat rebellious hair two or three pats, "and the reason is they had a ball game which ended in a norful row."

"You don't say!" cried the boy.

"Yes. There was four dollars and eighty cents up on the game, and our street won," went on the youthful chronicler. "And," she continued, "our boys got the money, all right."

"Well, why should there be a row, Alice?"

"It was this way," responded the child. "In the ninth inning our side was at the bat, and their team had already had their inning. They were two ahead of us. My brother Fred was our catcher, and he's told us about it at the table so often that I know it by heart. My brother went to bat first in that last half-inning, and he went out on a long fly. The next batter got his baste and stole second; the next batter got his baste on an error; and the next batter struck out; and then that easy-dropper, Johnny O'Brien—he's always listening to what folks are saying—came up and knocked a fly that should have been caught, but was muffed by the central fielder."

"The what?" cried the shocked Bob.

"The central fielder," returned Alice calmly and distinctly.

"Oh!" said Bob.

"Then my brother got busy. He wanted some of that money, and he wanted to beat that gang up on Ellen Street; and so, while Johnny O'Brien was running to first, and while the other two boys on the bastes were running in, he went up to the empire, who lives on Ludlow Street, and gave him a norful thump in the ribs. The empire has a bad temper; and that's what my brother was betting on. He turned round to see who struck him, and he started for Fred, and Freddie began backing away and sticking out his tongue at him. And while this was going on, Johnny O'Brien was running from first over to third. You see, he skipped second."

"But that wasn't fair," protested Bob.

"Wasn't it?" inquired Alice in a tone which indicated that no answer was expected. "Well, the other crowd just went wild: their catcher and pitcher ran in and caught that empire and turned him round, just as Johnny O'Brien came running in from third. My brother said that the ball was thrown in from the field in time to catch Johnny, but the catcher was too rattled to touch him in time. He only touched him as Johnny slid over the plate. Then my brother and the rest of the nine came at the empire before the other fellows knew what to

say, and yelled, 'How is it?' and the empire said, 'Safe."

"Caesar!" ejaculated Bob.

"And while the catcher and pitcher of the other team were punching the empire, my brother went over to the scorer and collected the four dollars and eighty cents."

"But that wasn't fair," protested Bob once more.

"My brother Fred," answered Alice, "says that they do it in professional games. He says that any player will cut the bastes if the empire isn't looking."

"That may be all right for professionals," said Bob, "but it's not real sport. Well, that was the reason for the row, was it?"

"Just part," responded the dear child.

"Did anything else happen?"

"Yes; while Fred was getting the money, the Kilgour Street shortstop grabbed our baseball mast."

"Mast?"

"Yes; you know what a mast is, don't you? The thing like a bird-cage that the catcher sticks his face into."

"I understand," said Bob gravely.

"And one of their other players got our ball, and the bat-carrier of their side got our new wagon-tongue bat. You wouldn't," continued

Alice, putting on an air of judicial severity, "think that Catholic boys, going to a Catholic school, would act like that, would you?"

"I—I—don't know," returned Bob.

"You don't? Why, that's stealing. All the boys on our street say so. They say that the Kilgour and Ellen Street crowd are nothing but out-and-out burgers."

"Burgers?"

"Yes, burgers. And they are burgers. I used to know most of them."

"Don't you know them yet?"

"When I meet them," answered the candid child, "I stick out my tongue at 'em."

"What do they do?"

Alice pouted.

"They say things about my hair."

"Like Johnny O'Brien?"

"Yes; they say it's pill-oxidized, whatever that means. And they mean it, while Johnny O'Brien doesn't. And it ain't. It just curls naturally." Here Alice paused, gave a gulp and added, "Almost."

"But what's all this got to do with me?" Bob asked.

"Just this: they've got our mast and ball and bat, and they won't give them up, and as long as they've got them no boy of their gang is safe on this street. We've got that four dollars and eighty cents, which we won fair and square, and as long as we've got it none of our boys dast go on their streets."

"But what have I got to do with it? I wasn't in that game."

"It's for everybody on the street. If you live on Pioneer Street it's enough."

"I don't see that at all," said Bob, "and so I'm going to see Albert Corcoran."

"Bob Ryan! Don't you do it. You'll get pounded. Suppose they give you a swollen lip: you wouldn't be able to smile 1"

"I'll chance it," returned Bob.

Visions of an unsmiling and swollen-faced Bob flashed before the inner eye of the infantile blonde. She caught Bob's arm in a gesture of entreaty, whereupon the bundle slipped and fell to the sidewalk. Four oranges rolled in various directions. Bob and Alice were quick to gather them.

"One of these," remarked the girl as she brought two oranges to Bob, "looks kind of funny. Part of it is too soft."

"I wonder how I came to buy that!" queried the boy. "It's no good."

"I'll tell you what, Bob: I'll take it myself if you really don't want it."

The child was young, frank, and without breakfast.

"Give it here," said Bob.

He took it, placed it on the top of the others, and presented his fair admirer with the biggest orange he had.

"Oh, thank you, Bob! Say, you're coming to my birthday party, aren't you?"

So occupied was Alice with the contemplation and the skinning of the welcome gift that when she raised her eyes again Bob was turning from Pike into Fifth.

"Oh," she said to herself, "he's gone and done it. They'll paradise him," she went on, misquoting one of her brother's favorite expressions.

Be it said to the credit of the infantile belle of Pioneer Street that she discontinued at once her operations on the orange and pattered back to her home, where she immediately took possession of the telephone, with the result that within five minutes every boy and every girl on Pioneer Street knew that the genial Bob Ryan was on his way to beard the lion in his den.

There were some rapid toilet performances that morning on the street, and before Bob had gone as far as Lock Street there was a gathering of the clans. Every member of the baseball team was there and about fifteen other boys. They assembled where Pike meets Pio-

20 HIS LUCKIEST YEAR

neer, and with grave faces entered into a council of war. A number of girls, looking too innocent to be trusted, hovered on the outskirts, taking no apparent interest in the proceedings, but with sharp ears intent to catch every word.

Bob meantime went briskly and blithely on. Turning south on Lock, he reached that wondrous up-hill thing called by courtesy "Little Fourth." The street was barely fifty feet long, but what it lacked in length it atoned for in steepness. It served as a thoroughfare to the pedestrian — and only the pedestrian — into Ellen Street.

Bob smiled as he began the ascent. The coast was clear. Very quickly, and breathing easily, he reached Ellen Street. It, too, as he thought, was deserted. Nevertheless, he was not unobserved. A young lady of twelve, Miss Mary Fitzgerald, her two stiff pigtails tied for the day, saw him from her room, and forthwith gave a gasp of dismay.

She knew Bob Ryan. Only a week ago she had dropped her books and stationery on Fifth Street, near the school, and Bob had sprung to her rescue. She still remembered his smile. She was a tomboy ; Bob Ryan she regarded as a good fellow. And here he was, unsuspecting youth, walking into the jaws of destruction*

"Why did those Pioneer people let him come?" she murmured. "Oh!" she added in dismay.

For just then out of the next house stepped jauntily William Devine, the catcher of the Ellen Street Ball Club, the best fighter of his age in the neighborhood, and the very boy who had thrashed the umpire, his senior by two years, on the memorable June day, some of the events of which have been so faithfully narrated by Alice O'Shea. It is only fair to say of Mary Fitzgerald that if it had been any other Pioneer Street boy she would have been the first to sound the alarm, the first, if need be, to lead the charge. But Bob Ryan had won her.

With bated breath she watched as William Devine issued from his gate and, turning, came face to face with Bob.

"Good morning," said Bob.

The face of William Devine went red as the comb of a turkey cock. He drew a long breath, stared, recovered himself, and said:

"You turn right round and beat it. I'll count three, and you start. If I catch you I'll pound you till your best friends won't know you."

"I'm not doing any running this morning," returned Bob pleasantly.

Waiting to hear no more, and forgetting to put on a shoe, the eager Mary Fitzgerald dashed through the house, and by some devious way known only to herself reached Lock Street and set off at top speed for Fifth.

There was a vision of flying pigtails and of imperfectly clad feet presently, which brought people to a standstill, while more than one uttered words to the effect that "that freckled-faced limb of Satan, Mary Fitzgerald, had broken out in a new place."

CHAPTER II

Bob, bearding the lion in Ms den, and in dire danger, invokes the dove of peace with startling results.

"1PVROP that bundle, and put up your

••—* hands," ordered William Devine.

Bob was still smiling.

"I am not fighting to-day, either," he answered.

There was nothing left for William but to give Master Bob Ryan the thrashing of his life. It was worth while doing too. William, though nearly fifteen, was a pupil of the seventh grade. He was, in the language of the school physician, "retarded." His development reflected more credit upon his body than upon his intellect. In all manner of athletic sports he stood second to none. William was well built, a trifle lighter than Bob, and unusually agile. He was far from being a bully, yet it is only fair to state that many and many a time he had "drunk delight of battle." As for the present adversary, there were rumors from the eighth-grade class that Bob Ryan was the strongest boy in the school. It was said that Bob was a good boxer and a

wonderful wrestler, and that, in spite of all this, he did not care about fighting. These rumors had been a source of annoyance to William Devine. They bade fair to rob him of a hard-earned prestige. Up to the time of Bob's arrival he had been recognized as the head of the school. Well, the occasion had happily arrived when the matter would for once and for all be settled.

William was firmly persuaded that when one fights one must be sure to get in the first blow. Bob had scarcely finished his sentence, when William struck out with all his force at the still smiling face. Up went both of Bob's hands—-in the left the package of oranges. That was the end of the package. Eleven oranges fell to the pavement and rolled their several ways. While they were rolling, something happened to William Devine which he has often wondered about since, trying vainly to account for it. His arms were pressed to his sides and kept there by another pair of arms; he was in the same second bent backward till he thought his bones would crack, and then Master William Devine, the hero of many a bout, found that he was flat on the sidewalk, with a hearty and heavy youth sitting astride him ; so seated that William could with difficulty move hand or foot.

It was a surprising discovery; it was all so sudden. William, lying face up to the sky, gave a shrill whistle. It was the call of the gang. Even as he whistled he looked into Bob Ryan's face with a glance which plainly showed admiration. Bob had conquered him in more senses than one.

There was a quick answer to the shrill call. Had there been an echo on Ellen Street it would not have died away before, baseball bat in hand, Master Edward Bolan issued forth from his house, some hundred-and-odd feet from the scene of the encounter. Edward was quick to take in the state of affairs. Uttering a warlike yell, he caught the bat in both hands and, with his gaze fixed on Bob, came forward at a dead run.

Bob's eyes ran over the oranges within his reach. There were three close at hand, and one was the very orange which the fair Alice had critized. Thanks to the strong fist of William Devine, it was pulpier than ever. He readjusted himself upon the prostrate body of his foe in such wise as to free his right hand, picked up the discredited orange, and, as young Bolan came within a few yards of him, let it fly with considerable force. It struck the eager and open-mouthed aggressor right

between the eyes, and brought him to a ludicrous halt.

Somehow, nevertheless, the sense of humor of the boys on Ellen Street was not aroused. Many of them, as they came thronging from their happy homes, viewed the orange-faced youth unsmilingly. In fact, they wasted no time in gazing upon the blinded victim, who looked and acted as though he had been struck by a bomb. With quickened feet they advanced and threw themselves upon Bob. In a few moments, not, however, before three of them had bitten the dust, Bob was a prisoner, held to the ground by six of the heaviest boys of the street, two for his legs, two for his arms, and two seated upon his person. William De-vine had taken no part in this scrimmage. He was stretching his arms and legs, and examining these extremities as though to assure himself that they were all there.

"Somebody get ropes," cried the lad who was holding on for dear life to Bob's right arm.

The smaller boys, meantime, who were too tender in years to give more than their moral support to the battle, had indulged in a wild scramble for the oranges. Ten of these youngsters were successful. Those who were empty-handed, having nothing else to do,

started off in various directions in quest of ropes.

By this time Edward Bolan was gazing once more with furious eyes upon a somewhat darkened world. Rushing forward, crying at the same time, "Let me at him," he was about to throw himself upon Bob. In his hand, instead of the discarded baseball bat, were the remains of the orange. With a fine sense of justice, Master Bolan's amiable intention was to give Bob a taste of his own medicine.

Between Bolan and his intended prey stepped quickly and resolutely William De-vine.

"No you don't, Ed Bolan," he said, catching that youth by the shoulders. "You don't hit no feller when he's down."

Just as Bolan opened his mouth to express indignation and other strong emotions, a very small boy, barefooted, hatless, and extremely out of breath, came running round the corner from Little Fourth Street.

"Cheese it! Cheese it!" he cried. He evidently had more to say, but his breath forsook him, and he paused, panting.

"Is it a cop?" asked Devine anxiously.

"No," gasped the runner. "It's the Pioneer Street bunch. They're coming."

There was a moment of silence and inde-

cision. Upon that silence broke the sound of many feet beating upon the stony irregularities of Little Fourth.

"If we let you free," asked Devine of the prostrate prisoner, "will you promise to keep out of this?" Devine needed the six captors for immediate service.

"I'll not fight, if that's what you mean," returned Bob Ryan. There was a slight abrasion under the husky youth's eye. The keeper of Bob's right arm had found it necessary to use a free-elbow.

"Loose him, fellers," commanded Devine, "and get ready for the Pioneer bunch."

Bob arose, stretched himself, dusted his clothes, and then all of a sudden broke into a smile. An idea had just come to him. The smile was still on his face when round from Little Fourth came the flower of the Pioneer Street youth, twenty strong, their first-line men, with Freddy O'Shea at their head. Bob was standing on the sidewalk alone. The Ellen Street youth of fighting age were massed in the middle of the street, awaiting the orders of their leader. Back of Bob stood ten youngsters of tender years, each grasping firmly an orange. Mixed with these were five others, each carrying his mother's clothesline. The remaining youth of the street were scurry-

ing hotfoot up to Kilgour to secure help for the royal battle now imminent.

On seeing their enemy a loud yell of hostile import arose from the flower of Pioneer Street. The flower then paused and formed into some sort of line. Evidently they were about to charge.

Then forth between the two massed fronts sprang Bob Ryan, and held up a hand that somehow seemed to be clothed in authority.

"One minute, boys," he called out in a strong, clear voice. "You fellows all belong to the Sodality, don't you?"

At least forty faces reflected forty varieties of disgust. To think of a fellow hauling in the Sodality on such an occasion—and the new Sodality at that! Only two weeks ago the working boys had been separated from those who attended school; worst of all, in the two groups thus questioned by Bob were at least twelve new officers. With a sinking heart William Devine reflected that he was sacristan. Before his mind's eye flashed two distinct pictures; one, of his lighting the candles as the boys filed in to the weekly meetings at St. Thomas' Church; the other, of his using his good right fist in darkening the vision of hia old enemy Freddy O'Shea. Each picture in itself was most comforting to his soul. But

closely associated, viewed thus together, they harrowed his whole being.

The reflections of Master Fred O'Shea, medal-bearer-elect of St. Aloysius Sodality, were strikingly similar. Both of these boys besides were agreed on this, that Bob Ryan had no sense of propriety.

Bob Ryan, looking upon the disgusted faces of friend and foe, realized for a few biting seconds —the first experience of the kind in his life —what it was to be unpopular.

"Of course, you're members," he went on, not without faltering. "Well, I'm the Sick Committee !"

"Johnny, Johnny," called a distant matron's voice, with the accent on the second syllable, prolonged and fully an octave higher than the first, "you come right home!"

Johnny showed no sign of having heard.

"The Sick Committee!" cried a host of inquiring voices.

"Yes. Last night Father Reardon, our Director, sent for me, and appointed me the Sick Committee, and told me to pay Albert Corcoran a visit. So I bought a dozen of oranges to bring him and "

Bob's speech was here interrupted, as ten small boys, with an alacrity no less creditable to their hearts than to their feet, crowded

about him, and pressed upon him as many oranges, which, strange as it may seem, were still intact.

"Why didn't you say so at first?" remonstrated William Devine. "We aren't angels upon this here street; but—" here William glared savagely upon his awe-struck followers —"I'd like to see any kid around here interfere with any officer of our Sodality when he's doing—when he's been—er—er '

"In the discharge of his duty," suggested Edward Bolan, who, one of the leaders of the eighth grade, happened to be the new Secretary.

"That's it," assented the virtuous William, "in the discharge of his duty. You just go ahead, Mr. Sick Committee, to see Corcoran; and if any kid on this street bats an eye at you I'll knock him silly."

"I'll bet he bought them oranges out of his own money," said Fred O'Shea. "That's the kind of a boy he is."

The faces so darkened by disgust a moment ago brightened into favoring glances upon the "Sick Committee" now going rapidly upon his errand of mercy.

Soon, however, there followed awkward moments. Visions of Sodality meetings clashed with prospects of a good fight, a settling of

ancient grudges. "Johnny" was now pleased to hear his mother's voice, and departed gladly homewards. Other youths heard similar voices: the Ellen Street crowd was melting away— all but the flower of the street, the first-line regulars. They really did not know what to do. Facing them, trying at once to remember that they were hostiles and So-dalists, stood the equally irresolute Pioneer Street warriors. What were they to do? Turn tail and run? That was against all their traditions. "Don't run till you know you're whipped," was their leading tenet. Were ever two groups of boys in quandary so sad?

The tension, just as Bob disappeared into the house where young Corcoran resided, was relieved by the appearance, at the head of Little Fourth Street, of the two young ladies, Alice O'Shea and Mary Fitzgerald.

"Good gracious!" ejaculated Freddy, "if my sister and Tomboy Mary aren't walking arm in arm like long-lost sisters."

What Freddy expressed everybody felt. The two girls had not been on speaking terms since an entertainment six months before, on which festive occasion Alice had sung a solo and Tomboy Mary had done the Buck-and-Wing. The singer had been encored once; the dancer three times. On the following day, at

school recess, Mary had called Alice's attention to the difference in the number of encores in undiplomatic language. Alice had answered back to the effect that if she had brought all her friends there the way Mary had done she would have gone on getting encores till the cows came home. From this the two dear children had proceeded to give their frank and unvarnished opinions, one of the other; after which they spoke no more. But now, as they appeared on Ellen Street, their vows of eternal friendship had been once more uttered. It was their common sympathy for Bob which had brought them together. Alice, a few minutes before, had managed to be on Fifth and Pike as the Pioneer Street boys had set out to Bob's rescue. She had seen the "did-dle-diddle-dumpling" girl, one shoe off and one shoe on, come flying up the street; she had heard Mary adjure the boys to hasten to Bob's rescue; and as they broke into a run, she had crossed over to the panting Mary and given her half of the orange—a half she had reserved for the first moment of leisure.

Before the vacillating armies could recover from their surprise at this vision of peace Alice called out:

"Look out, boys! Father Carney's coining up the street!"

That settled it. Lust of battle was completely dissipated. Everybody tried to look benevolent. The little hatless lad who had sounded the alarm heralding the advent of the "Pioneer Street bunch," called up to his sister on the second floor:

"M'rie, M'rie! trow down me hat—quick!"

She complied with comprehending sympathy. The youth put it on, and, as Father Carney passed, raised it with all the grace of a Spanish cavalier. He had no further use for the hat that day. It had served his purpose.

And as the Ellen Street boys followed the example of the quick-thinking youngster, the Pioneer Street force, not ungracefully, disappeared down Little Fourth Street.

"Good morning, boys," said Father Carney. "You look like a Sunday-school class."

"And that," muttered Master William De-vine, as he smiled at Father Carney, "is what I feel like. Confound itl"

CHAPTER III

Into the home of the Corcorans Bob Ryan brings the dove of peace.

A s Father Carney passed on serene and smil-•**- ing William Devine remarked:

"It's funny Father Carney didn't get on to us just now. He seems to think we were practising hymns or something."

"Oh, yes!" said Alice with a far-away look in her china-blue eyes.

"That's so," added Mary.

And then the two young ladies exchanged a flash of understanding, too telepathic in its nature for the cruder sensibilities of a mere male like William. As a matter of fact, it was they who, meeting Father Carney on Lock Street, had told the priest of the impending trouble. They say that women can not keep secrets. Nevertheless, they have the masonry of their sex, and it begins in tender years.

Bob Ryan was admitted into the Corcoran residence by the lady of the house, a short, stout, cheerful-faced woman, brisk in every movement, and with the clear olive complexion of the Italian.

"Good morning, boy."

"Good morning, ma'am," returned Bob with his smile unimpaired, "I'm the Sick Committee."

"Ah! glad to meet you. Shake hands, Mr. Sick Committee"; and Mrs. Corcoran gave Bob a cordial hand-clasp. "Is that your whole name?"

"It's my office, ma'am. My name is Bob Ryan."

"Oh," cried Mrs. Corcoran, in a voice that loudly proclaimed gladness and joy. "So it's you, is it, Bob Ryan? I've heard of you. Some of Albert's classmates have been here, and they like you, Bob."

"I'm mighty glad to hear that," returned the boy.

"Here, give me your hat. What in the world's the matter with your pockets? You're bulging as though you had the mumps all over you. Oh —oranges!"

"Yes, ma'am! I've come to see Albert, and, as he was sick, I thought he'd like a few oranges."

"I see," said the brisk lady, who, in the matter of smiles, was scarcely inferior to Bob. "And you're the Sick Committee for the boys' Sodality. I hope you'll like Albert."

"I'm sure I will," said Bob. "And if he's

anything like his mother I hope he'll like me. He'd be a friend worth having."

Loud and clear rang out Mrs. Corcoran's laugh.

"They told me you had kissed the Blarney Stone," she said. "I didn't believe them; but now I know it's true.— —Hey, Albert, here's Bob Ryan coming up to see you.— —This way, Bob; follow me. Watch out for these steps. There's a sharp turn."

Bob followed the light-footed, light-hearted mother up the stairs, and was ushered presently into the front room, spacious, well lighted, exquisitely neat, and made cheery with a riot of colors in the way of pictures and ornaments. The room was gypsy-like in richness of tone, Catholic in painting and statuary, and touched with rich Italian taste. To Bob's unsophisticated eyes it was lavishly furnished. And so it appeared to be; only a trained eye could perceive that it was a clear case of poverty in disguise.

Seated in bed was a boy of fourteen, dark-haired, dark-eyed, olive complexioned. Six weeks of fever had hollowed his cheeks, but had not not robbed him of his Italian beauty. His face was keenly intellectual. One who knew Italians would be inclined, on gazing upon him, to prophesy that one day he would

win distinction as painter or poet or metaphysician.

"Halloa!" cried Albert, extending toward Bob a wasted little hand. The greeting was simple; but the gesture, the eyes, the smile which accompanied the greeting clothed that poor word with the riches of the heart.

"Halloa!" returned Bob. "Why, you don't look sick at all."

"I'm not," answered Albert, taking Bob's measure with unconcealed appreciation. "I've heard the boys talking of you, and I was hoping you'd come."

"And I've heard them talking of you," said Bob; "and I've been just wanting to come the worst way. You were the leader of the seventh grade, they tell me; and all the fellows like you."

"Is that so?" snapped the mother. "It's a wonder they don't show it, then, by coming to see him. The only ones that have come near him are one or two boys on this street."

"It's this way, ma'am," Bob explained. "Boys are awfully fond of each other; but when one of 'em gets sick, they don't know what to do. Most of them can't sit down in a strange house and talk. But they mean all right."

"I remember," put in Albert, "when Olive

O'Rourke, who lives on Lock Street, got her foot smashed at the school-girls' party, when the radiator she was sitting on fell, that every boy and girl on Lock Street, and most of them on this street, called to see her the next day."

"Oh, that's different," said Bob. "She wasn't sick—she had a smashed foot. They all wanted to see that."

"And besides," added Mrs. Corcoran, "she had a five-pound box of candy, a sort of consolation prize. Jerry, the janitor, got Father Carney to give her that. But I believe you're right, Bob; a broken limb seems to have a special attraction for boys, and a corpse for girls."

"I'd be glad to have a little more company," said Albert, whose face was as radiant as his mother's, "but I don't care about breaking a leg for it."

Bob, a shade more radiant-faced than even mother and son, broke into a roar, in the which he was effectively joined by Mrs. Corcoran. Albert, out of sheer sympathy, followed with his own silvery laughter.

"You've brought sunshine into this room, Mr. Sick Committee," she said.

"It's coming in at the windows, ma'am."

"Not the sort of sunshine you carry with you. With you here, I think of Italian skies and the smile of God."

"Well, anyhow," continued the blushing Bob, "I've brought something." And out from his pockets and onto the table came the ten oranges.

"Oh, thank you. I'm very fond of oranges," said the convalescent.

"Do you like Albert?" queried the mother.

"Like him! Why, he's up to everything the boys have said of him, and more," answered Bob enthusiastically.

"So are you, Bob. And you are welcome in this house at any time; and for that matter, to anything in it. Now I'm going to work— five children and one husband keep a body hustling. By the way," the brisk woman went on, as she paused at the door, "you didn't have any trouble getting here, did you?"

"Nothing worth talking about, ma'am."

Mrs. Corcoran fastened her eyes sharply on Bob's disfigured cheek, and drew her own conclusions.

"Well, have a good talk; and the longer you stay, the more welcome you'll be. Good-by," and Mrs. Corcoran tripped down the stairs.

She did not, however, start to work at once. Opening the front door, she surveyed the street. All was quiet. But the street was not deserted. Within a few feet of the Corcoran residence stood a group of boys, prominent among them Edward Bolan and William De-vine. They were speaking in hushed yet evidently earnest tones.

"That confounded feud!" muttered the quick-eyed woman. "I suppose they're waiting for Bob Ryan—the little heathens!"

As though to confirm her suspicions, the group, on seeing her, became plainly agitated, particularly Edward, who slipped something at once with furtive haste into his pocket.

"Here, you boys, come this way. Quick," cried the Italian woman in incisive tones.

They shuffled forward, like culprits about to receive sentence.

"Look here," she continued. "Did you boys ever see me use a broom?"

"Oh, yes!" said the chorus.

"You did? Well, I know another way of using it; and if you boys dare to raise a hand on Bob Ryan when he leaves this house I'll show you the other way on your backs."

There was an awkward silence. The group looked pleadingly at William Devine, their leader.

"Please, ma'am," said William, speaking with no little difficulty, "I won't touch Bob Ryan. He's the Sick Committee."

"Oh!" said the lady with rising inflection.

"And he can lick me."

"Well!" gasped the lady.

"And he wouldn't when he could," continued the leader.

"Upon my word!" said the lady, in her tone an invitation for William to continue.

"And if anybody in these diggings lifts his hand against Bob Ryan," continued William, growing at once eloquent and free of speech, "I'll have it out with him myself."

"Then what are you boys waiting outside here for?"

Then up spake Edward Bolan.

"Please, ma'am, Bob Ryan spoiled an orange on me; and that orange was for Albert. I've got another one," he went on, dipping into his pocket, "and here it is."

Mrs. Corcoran managed to keep a straight face.

"Suppose you bring it up," she suggested.

"Go on, Ed."- -"That's the ticket."-"Yes, Ed; she's right." Thus did the crowd advise.

Looking like a doomed man on the way to the electric chair, Edward, orange in hand, shambled up the steps.

"Come along, Ed," said Mrs. Corcoran encouragingly, as she turned and led the way.

Then Edward did a strange thing. Slipping the orange under the good woman's arm, he turned and fled. He was seen no more that morning. Example is contagious. When Mrs. Corcoran turned to give some expression to a few of her feelings, she saw nothing but flying legs, and was presently gazing with a smile upon an utterly deserted street.

CHAPTER IV

Bob and Albert become friends, and, united, put an end to an ancient feud.

So you like Brother Cyril, Bob?" "Like him! That's not the word for it. Why, all of us like him. He's had us for three weeks now, and we all swear by him. And work! I should say we do— all except five or six. How can we help it, when he works so hard for us? There are twenty-four of us in the class of thirty-six who have made up our minds to try for a scholarship at St. Xavier College in the contest next June, open to all the eighth-grade classes of the city."

"Do they count me in?" asked Albert.

"Of course. Brother Cyril said he knew you were going to work for it, and he has talked up that contest till he's got us almost as interested as he is."

"It's too bad," commented Albert, "that our school can get only one winner. Last year Brother Cyril had three of his boys in the first five places. He got the first scholarship; but the second went to the cathedral, and the third, which should have gone to one of our boys, went to St. Edward's; the fourth to Coving-

ton, and the fifth, which should have been ours, too, to the Assumption Parish."

"Well, it's worth trying for whether a fellow wins or not. Every day after school most of us stay after class for an hour or more, and Brother Cyril keeps us busy. Then we've got our home tasks to do at night; and so we're kept going all the time."

"Don't some of the boys kick?" asked Albert.

"Not so that you can notice it. Why, it's all volunteer work; and the boys are interested. And they're jolly and good-natured. The only person who objected was a guardian of two of the boys. He was afraid his little charges would injure their health."

"That man ought to have been a woman," said Albert.

"I say, Albert," resumed Bob, after adjusting the pillows under the convalescent's head, "if you don't mind, I'll come over here every night and do my lessons with you."

"Why, that will be great!" cried Albert, sitting upright, and forgetting that he was still very weak.

"It will be for me," returned Bob. "Only I'm bound to say I won't be able to help you much in arithmetic. I'm pretty weak in that."

"So much the better," said Albert, as Bob

firmly pushed him back upon the pillows. "I'm strong in arithmetic, and can help you in that, and if I don't win the scholarship I hope you will."

"Then it's a bargain," said Bob, "and I'll be here to-morrow night. And when we get through our lessons I'll read to you. By the way, Albert, how is it that a boy with an Italian face like yours happens to have the name of Corcoran?"

"That is my father's name; but his face doesn't look like his name either: he's half Italian. My father is head bookkeeper in a big commission house, and he's got a mighty good salary; but when it comes to providing for a family of seven, the money seems to melt like butter at a picnic. My father is a wonder at figures. He's always calculating at something or other, even when he's home. He's mighty smart. And my mother can make a dollar go from here to San Francisco. Don't you like her, Bob?"

"I should say. She's quick as a flash, and jolly, and her smile is a real smile."

"She goes to five-o'clock Mass and communion every morning, Bob; and she's back in time to get us all up, and serve breakfast. She doesn't make any one else suffer on account of her piety. And I've a big brother of

seventeen who finished the St. Xavier business class last June. He's got a position at seven dollars and a half now; and it's a great relief to my mother. She doesn't have to scrape so much. His name is Angelo. He's working hard and expects to get a raise, and he's taking lessons from a private tutor four nights a week. Mother thinks he's working too hard; but he's very ambitious. Sometimes I'm afraid he'll break down. He's getting to look as thin as I am. But he's mighty good." "And what about the rest of your family?" "The rest? Oh, there's my three sisters, Josephine, Vera, and Rose. Josephine is in the first year of business at St. Xavier's: she's fifteen. Vera's in the sixth grade, and Rosie in the third. All three of them, when the weather is fine, go to six-o'clock Mass and communion. They're mighty nice sisters; but my mother has no end of trouble in keeping them nicely dressed. She can do as much with a needle as any woman in the parish; but she's always short of money; or rather, I should say, she used to be. My father gets one hundred and forty dollars a month; but somehow it never gets around. I can't make it out. Anyway, I am sure it's not his fault. He's always figuring and working at home. But now that my brother brings her his salary every week,

mother hasn't any trouble to speak of at all."

"I think," said Bob, "that I ought to tell you something about myself. So far as I know I have neither brother nor sister; I have no remembrance of my mother, who died when I was a baby, and my father disappeared over two months ago."

"That's pretty hard," murmured Albert sympathetically.

"Well, anyhow, I've lots of friends; and, what's more, I believe I'm getting another good one to-day." And Bob looked Albert straight in the eyes.

"I believe you are," answered Albert, catching Bob's hand.

"I suppose," continued Bob, "you've heard about our Sodality."

"Why, yes, Bob. They tell me that I'm librarian."

"Yes, you are; but you needn't worry about your work, because we haven't a library yet. I think it was a good move to make the old Sodality into two —one the St. Stanislaus for the working boys, and one the St. Aloysius for the school boys. There are one hundred and twenty in our Sodality now, and thirty of them are officers. Father Reardon says we're pioneers, and if we make a good start the Sodality will keep on going for years."

"How about your being the Sick Committee, Bob? I never heard anything of that till you came in."

"I'll tell you about that, Albert. Last week, at our meeting, Father Reardon said he'd like to get suggestions from any member with regard to Sodality work. It occurred to me that we ought to have a sick committee, and I told him; and so last night he sent for me, said it was a great idea, and appointed me."

"It is a fine idea," exclaimed Albert.

"And when he appointed me Sick Committee, he gave me your address. So I started out this morning; and it was the Sodality that got me here safely. When the boys here had captured me, and the Pioneer Street kids came rushing to my help, I just settled everything by saying I was the Sick Committee. That settled it." 1

"They're still fighting about that ball game, are they?"

"Yes; sort of foolish, isn't it?"

"And I understand that near half of the officers belong to this street and Pioneer. They have to sit together at the meetings. There's something wrong about it."

"Say, Albert, can't we settle that feud?"

"You can, Bob, I believe."

"How?"

There was a long conference between the two; then Devine and Bolan were sent for and interviewed. Those two leaders departed wearing broad grins.

On leaving Albert, Bob found three raven-haired daughters of Italy, all ribbons and smiles, awaiting him downstairs. They were really nice children, these sisters of Albert's, bright and beautiful, and typically Italian. Bob became their friend on sight.

To the astonishment of some one-hundred-and-twenty-odd families living on the streets from Ellen to Pioneer, Bob Ryan walked all the way arm in arm with Bolan and Devine. The dove of peace seemed to be hovering over the happy trio.

It was Alice and her dearest friend in the world since the day before, Elizabeth Reno, who, espying them from afar, gave notice of their coming.

At Fifth and Pike—neutral territory—the group was broken. Leaving the protagonists of Ellen Street there, Bob proceeded to Pioneer Street. Presently he was in heated controversy with Johnny O'Brien and Freddy O'Shea. It took these earnest youths some time to understand that the Pioneer boys had not been good sports, that things might be done in professional games which should not

be tolerated in amateur contests. Fred Q'Shea grew angry; but Bob remained calm.

"Well, anyhow," said Johnny O'Brien, "we want to be fair and square. Perhaps we weren't."

"And we are fair and square," retorted Fred. "The Ellen Street club didn't win. Why should we give them that money?"

"And besides," added Johnny, veering once more to his leader's opinion, "they stole our masks and bat and ball."

"You're right, Fred," said Bob, "they didn't Win."

"Well, then, what the dickens are you fussing about?"

"Why, just this," returned Bob. "They didn't win, and neither did you."

"But we did."

"Yes, by a trick, if you call that winning. But I don't think you've a right to take other people's money on a trick like that."

"It's all very well for you to talk, Bob Ryan; you weren't in that game. It isn't any of your funeral anyhow."

"In one way it isn't, Fred. But then you see I'm thinking about the Sodality."

At the word "Sodality," the air of ferocity on Fred's face disappeared with magical effect. He saw himself in fleeting vision passing

around the medals to the Sodality on the coming Sunday, and his face became obsequious to his thought.

"How," continued Bob, "are we officers to work together, if we have to pretend being friendly? It's not right. We'll not do things. We'll never be the banner Sodality."

The word "banner" had an extraordinary effect on Fred. If the Sodality had any life in it, there would surely be a procession some sweet day, and he as medal bearer would be the privileged one to carry the banner. Waves of piety passed over his face; he was looking just then as he hoped to look when the great occasion arrived.

"Well, Bob, what have you got to propose?"

By this time the three youths were surrounded by the children of the street. There were no laws of privacy in the bright lexicon of Pioneer Street.

"Just this: we'll call the game a draw."

"Yes; and what then?"

"We'll give the Ellen Street people their money back."

"What! All of it? Why, two dollars and forty cents of it was ours."

"I said 'their money,' two dollars and forty cents," continued Bob. "And they'll give us back our mask and ball and bat."

"That sounds fair," said Fred slowly.

"It'll make us good sports," added Johnny O'Brien proudly.

"But hold on!" Fred continued. "Those kids have had our ball and bat and mask, and used them."

"Just so," put in an onlooker. "They ought to allow us something for wear and tear."

"Suppose we take out one dollar," suggested Fred.

"Not enough!" cried several.

"Too much!" said a few.

"Of course," said Bob, "we ought to be allowed something for wear and tear; but I don't think it's fair for us to be the judges."

"Right-o," assented Johnny O'Brien. "If we're going to be sports, let's be good sports."

"Well," argued Fred, "you don't want them to be the judges, do you?"

"No; that wouldn't be right either," admitted Bob.

"Suppose we put it up to the Chief of Police," suggested Johnny O'Brien's younger brother.

"You go and chase yourself around the block," cried Johnny.

Even the little girls cast eyes of disapproval upon the youthful O'Brien, who very quickly departed to console himself with a penny's worth of candy.

"How about Father Carney or Father Reardon?" suggested another.

"But they don't know anything about our row," said Fred. "And why should they? It wouldn't interest them."

"Oh, no!" put in the fair Alice. "Father Carney shouldn't know anything about it."

Miss Mary Fitzpatrick gazed with unconcealed admiration upon the fair Alice, who at that moment looked as though she were posing for a picture of Innocence.

"I'll tell you what, boys," cried Freddy in a burst of inspiration. "We'll put it up to the Sporting Editor of the Enquirer."

Fred became for the moment the hero of the street.

"The next thing," continued Fred, still riding on the wave of popularity, "is to collect some of that money that's been divided up among the fellers. We'll sure need at least one dollar and fifty cents."

Freddy's popularity, at least among the ball players, dropped like a stick. Several of the team, looking thoughtful, unostentatiously disengaged themselves from the crowd and went their various ways.

"I'll put in a quarter," continued Fred, who

a moment before had resolved to donate but ten cents to the cause.

"Put me down for another," added Bob.

"And me for twenty cents," said Johnny O'Brien. "Let's all be good sports."

It was the ambition of Tomboy Mary's life to be a good sport. She gave over her only nickle. Alice, too, had aspirations in the same way, expressed in the sum of three cents.

Within five minutes the sum was collected.

On that same afternoon the Sporting Editor of the Enquirer received with perfect gravity a delegation of youths, nine in number, who, with as little explanation as they could possibly give, wanted to get the valuation on the wear and tear of a bat and ball and catcher's mask.

It took half an hour to settle the matter at eighty-five cents; and, as the Editor insisted on paying that sum out of his own pocket, the peace committee found itself with nearly one dollar on its hands.

It was Johnny O'Brien who suggested a celebration in the form of fireworks. Johnny, now the dead-game sport of Pioneer Street, carried his point.

On Sunday morning there were in the Enquirer two articles concerning our young friends. The first was in the sporting column,

and announced that the St. Aloysius Ball Team was already organized for the coming spring, and was open to challenge from any club of boys not over sixteen in Cincinnati or vicinity. Frederick O'Shea was its captain, William Devine its catcher, and Edward Bo-Ian its shortstop. Its pitcher, the article went on to declare, was the best twirler of his age in the city, Master Robert Ryan, whose control was almost perfect.

"Almost perfect," exclaimed Edward Bo-Ian, as he read the article and passed his hand over his eyes, "I should say it is."

The other article was among the locals, and read as follows:

A Belated Fourth of July.

Johnny O'Brien Celebrates.

Doctor Says It's Not Serious.

"Last night Johnny O'Brien, aged 13, of 836 Pioneer Street, for the delectation of his youthful friends and admirers, undertook to shoot off a giant firecracker. Johnny held it a moment too long. His hand was burned, and he is now considering taking a week's vacation from school. Johnny looks forward to his absence with fortitude. In justice to him, he bore his pain without flinching, and his friends on the street unanimously pronounce him a sport."

Thus in one day died out forever an ancient feud, from the ashes of which arose a live Sodality with a ball team the like of which, tender age considered, had never before flourished in St. Xavier Parish.

CHAPTER V

The Flower Section is organized, and begins its promising career with a case which still involves a mystery.

A FTER the events set down in the first four •*•• chapters of this chronicle there was no further question of Bob Ryan's standing in St. Xavier School. His feat in sitting upon and holding down William Devine for nearly five minutes settled the vexed question as to his being the strongest boy in the eight grades; his triumph of marksmanship in bringing Edward Bolan, bat in hand, to a full stop by a hand-grenade in the shape of a pulpy orange led to his being tried out and selected as pitcher for the great St. Aloysius ball team; while his tact and judicial poise in putting an end to a feud of over three months* duration stamped him in the eyes of parents and children as a second Daniel come to judgment. Best of all, his introduction of the Sodality as a factor into questions of everyday life gave new vigor and impetus to that promising organization.

The Sick Committee became a household word. The Children of Mary, of which Sodality both Miss Alice O'Shea and Miss Mary

Fitzgerald were shining ornaments, took up, at the instance of Alice, the question of starting a similar section. They called it The Flower Section, and Alice with Elizabeth Reno, the girl who just then happened to be her bosom friend—an intimacy that had lasted unbroken for five days and a half—were appointed the Flower Section Committee by their Director, Father Carney, with the privilege of choosing a third member. They at once hit upon Mary Fitzgerald, in consequence of which choice seven of their dearest friends on Pioneer Street refused to speak to them for fully a week. Those girls had local pride. The appointment to office had a wondrous effect on the tomboy of Ellen Street; she walked, when conscious of her office—and she was conscious of it in most of her waking hours —with a certain attempt at dignity, and gave up forever her artless habit of sticking out her tongue at persons with whom she did not fully agree. Her first act, on receiving news of her appointment, was to buy a dozen oranges, armed with which and dressed in her Sunday best she came down upon Alice O'Shea in her proper home, and inquired what girl in the Children of Mary Sodality was ill.

Alice's blue eyes opened to their widest. She shook her flaxen curls. Yes, flaxen curls!

The readers of this simple tale were introduced to the fair child in deshabille. They saw her on Saturday morning. Little girls, like their older sisters, are at their best, in point of appearance, in the afternoon. And on the particular afternoon when Mary —no longer the tomboy of Ellen Street, but a flower-girl — paid her a visit, Alice was gay, as to her hair, with ribbons, and arrayed in stockings fully as white as her conscience, with slippers to match both, and a white dress set off in all its immaculateness with a blue sash. A shining bracelet on one wrist gave the child the finishing touch.

"Why, Mary," returned Alice, "there is no one sick that I know of."

"That's too bad," said Mary, with genuine regret in her voice. "I bought these oranges for her. You see, I had fifteen cents which some lady gave me for going on an errand for her; and I was afraid if I didn't buy the oranges right away I might spend the money.'*

Alice stood for full three seconds in deep reflection.

"I'll tell you what," she then said, "I'll call up Elizabeth Reno. She's just as anxious as we are to have a sick member. Maybe she's found one."

Then Alice took up the receiver.

"Is that you, Elizabeth? Do you know who this is?—you don't?—Well, you needn't get sassy about it.—Hey?—What's that?—Yes, this is Alice, and I miss you so much—the same as you miss me. Say, come on over.— Yes, right away.—Oho, I'm so glad you've got your white slippers on. It's too bad your hair is bobbed, because we could both have curls if it weren't.—Say, Mary Fitzgerald is here, and she's brought along a bundle of oranges for a sick girl; and we've just got to find a sick girl before those oranges spoil or get eaten.— All right, Elizabeth, come right over."

When ihe eager Elizabeth arrived she was greeted with fervent "halloas" from the other two members of the Flower Section.

Together they went over the membership list of the Children of Mary. It was a great disappointment to them that every girl on the roster could be accounted for as in daily attendance at school.

"Why, just think," exclaimed Alice, "there's that skinny, dough-faced Annie Morrison who was sick more than half of last year with ammonia and newrology; and this year she hasn't missed a day."

"It's a shame!" observed Elizabeth.

"I wished she'd put it off till this year," remarked the Flower of Ellen Street.

"Say," Alice went on, "maybe Father Carney knows some girl who's sick. I think I'll telephone him."

"Maybe he wouldn't like it," Elizabeth objected.

"But isn't it our duty?" answered Alice.

"And, besides, I don't want my oranges to spoil," observed Mary.

At this point of the conversation Alice, happening to notice something in the attire of Elizabeth which appealed to her aesthetic sense, proceeded to remark upon it, whereupon the three young ladies forgot for full ten minutes the affairs of the Sodality in the absorbing question concerning what they were to wear on the following Sunday. The conversation became more than absorbing, when, in a happy moment, Mary Fitzgerald, the regenerate, suggested that the Flower Committee adopt a uniform. The Red Cross nurse attire was discussed, and finally rejected on the grounds that the Children of Mary Sodality ought to have something different.

They took up the question of hair-ribbons. Elizabeth, somewhat dark of complexion, came out strong for red; fair-haired Alice, for reasons clear to every girl, stood staunch for blue. The conversation reached a point where Elizabeth, risen to her feet and with eyes flash-ing, was about to inform her dearest friend in the world that she would never speak to her again, when the telephone rang.

Alice took up the receiver:

"Halloa!—Oh, is it you, Mrs. Reno?— What?—Catherine has gone to bed!"

There was a pause; then—

"All right; I'll tell Elizabeth at once. Good-by."

Then Alice turned, all trace of the late vexation gone from her expressive features.

"Oh, Elizabeth, your sister Catherine has took sick and has gone to bed with a side-splitting headache."

At the announcement Mary Fitzgerald fairly beamed with joy. Elizabeth was pleased, too, though her pleasure was somewhat alloyed, as shown by an air of perplexity and a wrinkled brow.

"I'm glad," said Mary, "that our first sick girl to be visited by this here committee is a sister of one of the flowers, and a seventh-grade girl at that."

Then as one man up rose the Flower Section, and arm in arm fared forth into the street.

"Who's sick?" called Johnny O'Brien, with his usual intense interest in everybody else's interest. His right hand was swathed in ban-

dages to the size of a pillow; but John in face was as serene as ever.

Before the three fragrant flowers, having vouchsafed the desired information, had crossed the street and progressed the fifty feet or so which stood between the respective houses of the O'Sheas and the Renos, everybody on Pioneer Street, except old Mrs. Boylan, who was stone deaf, were discussing the fact that Catherine Reno was down with a "side-splitting" headache.

Mary Fitzpatrick, indeed, was alarmed. Not so Elizabeth, for that fair flower distinctly remembered that before leaving her home she had informed her sister Catherine that the Flower Section had a dozen oranges on hand, and were going to get together to see whether they could not find some sick child of Mary upon whom to lavish them.

Their first visit of mercy was a success. Catherine listened to their prattle with patience, and accepted the oranges, after Mary had overcome all her apparent objections. During the visit it was also settled that the three flowers should wear in their official work any color of hair-ribbon they chose.

Hard upon their departure Master Johnny O'Brien, with that whole-hearted interest he took in everything connected with Pioneer

Street, engaged Elizabeth in friendly talk. Tt was easy for Johnny to get out of the unsuspecting flower every detail that had led up to Catherine's sudden illness. All this within due time—that is, within the next five minutes —Johnny faithfully retailed to his boy friends. Their curiosity was aroused.

After supper Johnny visited the invalid and talked to her for half an hour, during which time he watched her closely. Then he bade her a friendly adieu, expressing the hope that she would be quite well in the morning; a hope, by the way, which was fully realized.

"Well," cried Fred, speaking in the name of every boy on the street as Johnny came out^ "is she really sick?"

All waited with undisguised interest for Johnny's reply.

Johnny paused, raised his heroic hand, heroic in size and in history, on high, and answered:

"You can search me!"

Whether the gifted young lady, who shared her oranges with her sister, giving her one, was really ill or not on this occasion is a mystery which no one has as yet solved.

CHAPTER VI

The strange conduct of Mr. Corcoran, and the mysteries attendant upon his giving up work forever.

To do justice to the Flower Section, they showed subsequently great zeal and did really good work in their dealings with the sick members of the Children of Mary. They were lucky in having before their eyes an excellent model, Master Bob Ryan. That young gentleman had a genius for dealing with people in sorrow and distress. In a few weeks he was looked upon by the Corcoran family as one of themselves. Every evening without fail he visited Albert, and together they went over the next day's lessons to their mutual benefit. Bob was strong in English; Albert in mathematics.

During these days Bob came to know Mr. Corcoran and Angelo. Mr. Corcoran was a puzzle to the boy. He was a dark man, with very gentle, dreamy, black eyes, and a fierce moustache, long, blue-black, and curled upward at the ends. His face, in other words, was a contradiction—ferocious below, lamblike above.

Mr. Corcoran in his own household seldom spoke. His thoughts seemed ever to be far away. Sometimes Bob wondered whether he really knew his own children by name. At meals he occasionally broke into speech; and ever he spoke of a day soon to come when the family would leave Ellen Street and move to Clifton.

"I've got my eye on a dwelling there," he said one day in Bob's presence, "which is worth one hundred thousand dollars, and it's going begging for forty thousand. I'm going to buy that."

Mrs. Corcoran smiled—almost any remark drew a smile from her—but said nothing. The children listened with sparkling eyes. They had perfect faith in their father. They considered him to be one of the most wonderful men alive.

"I say, pa," Albert objected, "how can you pay forty thousand for a house on a salary of one hundred and forty dollars a month?"

Mr. Corcoran's eyes put on a far-away look.

"Forty thousand dollars 1" he cried. "Ah, bah! that's nothing. You needn't worry about money, children. In a short time you'll have more than you'll know what to do with. And my salary—that's nothing. Very soon I shall work for no man."

Then Mr. Corcoran, forgetting to take the quarter of pie just handed him by his wife, and leaving his cup of tea untouched, arose and departed hastily for his "den"—a little cubby-hole on the second floor at the head of the landing.

"I wonder," said Angelo, "what father's got up his sleeve."

Mrs. Corcoran ceased smiling as she said, not without a touch of sweetness in her tone—

"Angelo, that doesn't sound very nice. You are speaking of your father."

"Beg pardon, mother; we do get careless the way we talk. What I should have said is: 'what plan my father has.' He certainly has something on his mind. And I know he's working on something."

Bob was looking earnestly at Mrs. Corcoran. That good woman bent her head low for a moment, and it seemed to the sharp-eyed boy that a spasm of pain passed over her face. The next moment she raised her eyes and smiled brightly.

"If I thought, children," she said, "that wealth would make you better and happier, I'd pray for it every day. But I don't, and so I'm content to say just 'Give us this day our daily bread.'"

"I'd rather pray for cakes," said Rosie.

And the supper party then broke up in riotous laughter.

As Bob helped the still weak Albert up the stairs he could not help noticing Mr. Corcoran seated before a table. The man was apparently checking off numbers. Sheets of paper were all about him, on all o j theni combinations of numbers and letters.

Two hours later Bob, leaving for the night s saw Mr. Corcoran once more. He was still engrossed with his mysterious work.

So had it been every night. Mr. Corcoran always worked with the door open; but into that den no one but himself was supposed to enter. From the time that he entered his den there was perfect quiet in the house. Singing or loud talking was absolutely forbidden. Indeed, for the last four or five weeks Mrs. Corcoran had not been permitted to run her sewing machine. No wonder that Bob Ryan was puzzled.

Angelo was like his father in his gift for quick figuring; like his mother in energy and sprightliness. His salary had been raised twice in a month. He was now getting ten dollars a week, and there was promise of his soon being promoted to the office of assistant bookkeeper, with a substantial increase. And Angelo was working for it. Every night he

either studied at home or went to take instruct tions from his private tutor. Seldom did he retire until midnight; but always before his father, who, intent on his mysterious occupation, burned the midnight oil not unfrequently into the first flicker of the dawn.

To Bob's joy, the time soon came when Albert was able to get about ; and for twelve days before his return to school he transferred his place of studies from his proper home to his new friend's delightful room.

At ten o'clock, their lessons thoroughly prepared, the two walked arm in arm as far as Little Fourth Street. Arrived at that ascent, it was Master Bob's custom to catch Albert in his strong arms and to carry him up to the level.

On the last night of October the two reached the foot of the street that was steep.

"Well, Bob," said Albert, "you needn't carry me to-night. I don't feel a bit tired; and to-morrow I start to school."

"Fine," said Bob, taking his friend's arm. "Come on, now, and don't be afraid to lean on me. Oh, but the boys will be glad when you get back. They all say that as soon as you start in I won't be the leader any more. They say you can beat me all hollow; and I believe them."

"Well, I don't," returned Albert. "You've got more English in your little finger than I have in my whole head.—Halloa! What's the matter? If that isn't my father standing on the front steps! What's happened to him and his den? I never knew him out of it at this time of night in the last six months."

"Halloa, boys!" cried Mr. Corcoran, motioning for them to come near.

"Good evening, sir," said Bob.

"Well, boys, everything is fixed. I've left my position."

Mr. Corcoran's eyes were shining. His face was that of an ecstatic. The heavy lines under his eyes, brought on by want of sleep, had disappeared. He looked ten years younger.

"I've been working," continued the man, with an air of exaltation, "for nine months without intermission. And I've got it!"

"Got what, pa?"

"To-morrow," continued the father, "I take my first holiday and start my fortune."

"Are you going to be rich, pa?"

"I am rich." Here the man placed his hand over his coat pocket. "There's over one hundred thousand dollars in value here right now. We'll move to Clifton by the first of next week. On the day after to-morrow I buy the

house there. And, Angelo" — here Mr. Corcoran paused and looked at his large-eyed son -"that is—eh— Albert, you'll never want money as long as you live."

Saying this, Mr. Corcoran, holding his hand tightly over his pocket, turned and walked into the house.

"Good gracious, Bob, what do you make of it?" cried Albert after a prolonged pause.

"I'm sure I don't know," answered Bob.

"Well, Bob, I don't either; but if I get lots of money we're partners."

And the boys shook hands for the night.

It was nearing four o'clock on the afternoon of the following day. St. Xavier School had been dismissed. Only the chosen boys of the eighth grade had remained. Brother Cyril was explaining to these alert and ambitious youths the thing they call in English the nominative absolute. Very soon every one present grasped the explanation.

The boys were a set worth studying. There was perfect discipline in the room. And yet many a man would have said that there was none at all. For the young students were cheerful to a striking degree, and free in their remarks to the teacher and to one another. There appeared to be no rule of silence. There was, too, no little good-natured badinage.

And yet there was perfect discipline; because Brother Cyril could do with these boys what he pleased.

While these merry youngsters were composing out of hand sentences rich in nominative absolutes and hurling them into one another's teeth, Brother Cyril raised his hand.

"Take out your paper," he said.

How quickly the execution followed upon the command!

"Now write seven sentences, each one with a nominative absolute; and let there be perfect quiet."

For five minutes the scratching of pens was the only sound; and then—there came a knock at the door.

Brother Cyril opened it himself. A policeman was standing outside. Of the twenty-four boys present only three raised their eyes and glimpsed the strange visitor. Brother Cyril closed himself out, and for several minutes more the only sound in that classroom continued to be the scratching of pens.

When Brother Cyril returned, his face was quite pale; and a close observer would have noticed a slight quivering of the lips.

"Albert Corcoran," he said quietly, "I want to speak to you for a moment."

The boy arose promptly and followed his teacher outside the classroom.

"I'm awful sorry for you, my boy," said the Brother as he closed the door, "but there's bad news."

"Oh, has anything happened to my mother?"

"No, she's as brave a woman as I've ever met; and the bad news has come to her as well as to you. It's your father."

"Oh, Brother, he hasn't done anything wrong, has he?"

The poor boy was thinking of his father's strange conduct. In spite of himself his imagination at once grew alive with vague suspicions.

"No, my boy, there is nothing like that, thank God. He was over in Kentucky this afternoon and fell unconscious on a street in Ludlow."

"And — and—is he dead, Brother?"

"He came to after a few minutes," continued Brother Cyril, "and gave his name and address. And then one of the priests over there arrived and got his confession and anointed him, when he became unconscious again. But before he lost his senses he gave the priest a message for your mother alone."

"I'm awful glad he got a priest," said the

boy. "You see, my father's been so busy working out something or another that he's been careless. I'm sure he didn't mean to be. We've all been praying for him—Oh, you needn't tell me, Brother; I know he's dead."

Here the boy broke down.

"You must be brave, Albert," continued the Brother, "for the sake of your mother and your sisters."

"I will—I will," raising his head and standing erect. The next moment he collapsed.

"Bob," cried Brother Cyril, holding Albert in one arm and opening the door of the eighth-grade class a few inches, "come this way at once."

Bob Ryan showed no surprise. He simply took Albert in his sturdy arms, carried him to the water faucet near at hand, threw a few drops of water on the deathly pale face, and with a caressing hand rubbed the brow. In the meantime Brother Cyril related briefly the story of Mr. Corcoran's sudden death.

"He died with the sacraments, Albert," whispered Bob into the ear of Albert.

Albert opened his eyes.

"I'm sure," added Bob, "that he died a good death."

"We've all been praying for six weeks that he might," whispered Albert. "The girls have

been going to communion every day, and Angelo went when he could. My mother asked us to. She told us she was alarmed about him. I believe that our prayers have been heard."

"Brother Cyril," said Bob, 'Til take Albert home."

Two days later the funeral took place. Mrs. Corcoran had contrived to keep up a small insurance policy on her husband's life, enough to pay the expenses of the obsequies. She had received the message to her from the priest. But of that message she said nothing. Neither did she tell any one that, although her husband had received his full salary the day before his death, not one cent of it ever reached her hands or was ever accounted for in any way soever.

CHAPTER VII

In which Bob starts something really worth while.

AY, Bob," said Albert, bursting into Bob's room without the formality of knocking, "I've got good news."

"Good! What is it?"

"Angelo's been promoted. He's simply a wonder at figuring, like my poor father we buried two weeks ago, and they've made him assistant bookkeeper at sixty dollars a month."

"Just think!" exclaimed Bob, "and he finished from our business class only a little over four months ago."

"Do you know what that means to us, Bob?" continued Albert, throwing himself into a chair.

"What?"

"Why, it means just this: My mother doesn't have to worry about the rent or the bills any more. Sixty dollars! Why, she never had that much money each month since I can remember. Sixty dollars will go as far with her as a hundred with most women. She wastes nothing. I've often wondered what

became of my father's salary."

"Do you know," said Bob, "that fathers are queer propositions? At least, that's the way it seems to me. Mine was funnier than yours."

"He was?"

"I should say. He wasn't very kind, and he hardly ever spoke to me; and, while he had lots of money, he gave me very little, and last summer he took me out into a woods, and told me to clear out, and to change—oh, I came near forgetting! I'd like to tell you all about him, Albert; but I don't think I've a right to. Anyhow, I left him and he left me, and I don't know what's become of him nor why he acted the way he did; and the whole thing's a mystery that's bothering me and a lot of my friends."

"And you're worse off than I am, Bob— you have no mother."

Bob had the reticence of the normal American boy. But, had he spoken what he felt, he would have told Albert that whenever he met Mrs. Corcoran the pain of longing for a loving mother, a mother like Albert's, almost brought the tears to his eyes.

"Anyhow," he said, "I've no cause to whine. I've got the best friends any boy could wish to have, including your mother, Albert. I've friends in our class, and friends on our street, and friends scattered along the banks of the

Mississippi. A fellow can't expect to have everything. And Tom Temple and the Reades are on the lookout to find what's become of my father and why he sent me adrift."

"We're awfully happy about our brother's raise," Albert went on, "and we've been thinking, my mother and sisters and I, what we ought to do."

"Well, did you settle it?"

"Not entirely, Bob. But one thing we've fixed on: we're going to receive communion every day, in thanksgiving."

Suddenly Bob's eyes grew bright.

"By George, Albert," he exclaimed, "you've given me an idea! You go to communion every day; so do I, at the five-thirty Mass I serve. Then there's a lot of the acolytes who go daily, too. Why can't we get up a Communion Section in our Sodality, the same as the young ladies?"

"How do you mean, Bob?"

"Just this. Let's try to get every boy of the Sodality in it. Of course we can't get all to go daily; but some can go twice a week, others three times, and almost any boy can go at least once. If they do that much they can be members."

"That looks good to me," said Albert.

"It will stop a whole lot of sin," continued

80 HIS LUCKIEST YEAR

Bob. "A boy who receives once a week isn't likely to go wrong. You put my name down, and I'll get all the boys on this street to go in on it, and I'll tell Brother Crellin, the sacristan, to-morrow to get the altar boys interested."

"But why don't you get it up yourself, Bob?"

"Who, me? That's your little offering of gratitude. You can do it; and I know you'll like to do it."

"Yes; but you'd like to do it, too."

"But I'm the Sick Committee. I've six boys on hand now. And another's at the Betts Street Hospital. They take up pretty much all of my spare time."

"All right, Bob; it's a go. I'm sure, too, that Father Reardon will like it."

"Of course he will," said Bob. "I heard him talking the other day about our eighth-grade boys. He said that most of them were just at the dangerous age, when boys begin to get bad habits if they're not mighty careful. And then he said something I don't intend to forget."

"What was it?"

"He said that there were two things which were dead sure to keep Sodality boys of fourteen and fifteen out of mortal sin; and that Brother Cyril had settled one of them for his boys, and that he, the director of the Sodality, ought to contrive to bring about the other."

"What two things, Bob?"

"One was to keep the boys busy—keep 'em playing and studying hard, with no time for loafing. And Brother Cyril has attended to that."

"He certainly has," said Albert.

"And the other things," went on Bob, with an enthusiasm which showed on every feature, "is frequent, and, if possible, daily communion. And he said that if he could get the boys to doing that he'd be perfectly happy."

"Say, Bob, let's surprise him. I'll tell you what I'll do: I'll get after these boys myself —all but the bunch you said you'd attend to; and I'll give every minute of my spare time to seeing them; and when I've got the list made out I'll bring it to Father Reardon."

"Fine," cried Bob. "It ought to be fixed up inside of ten days."

"And we'll put one over on the Children of Mary," added Albert boyishly.

I am afraid Albert reckoned without his host. Johnny O'Brien got wind of the affair early the next day. Hot with the news, he reported it to Fred O'Shea, who at once declared that he'd join and go to communion at least three times a week—which to Master

Fred was a somewhat radical change. No one appreciated this fact more than himself. In fact, he began to put on airs; and boasted at table of the great Communion Section.

Leaving her breakfast unfinished, the fair and eager Alice telephoned her dearest friend in the world, Elizabeth Reno, repeating her brother's remarks almost verbatim. Not entirely, however. Elizabeth had some trouble in understanding that the St. Aloysius Sodality was getting up a "Eucalyptic" Section.

"And," added Alice, "I think we ought to do something."

"Of course we ought," came Elizabeth's decided tones through the receiver, "only we've got to get another name. Eucalyptic Section sounds funny; and the girls in the fifth grade won't be able to pronounce it."

"Oh, I don't care what we call it," answered Alice sweetly. "We ought to get another name anyhow."

"Listen, Alice," came the voice of the dearest friend. "Just hold the phone for a second. Catherine's here, and she won't let me talk to you till I tell her all about it."

There was a silence for several minutes. Then-

"Oh, Alice! My sister thinks it's lovely; and she got just the beautifullest name; and she's made it up out of her own head. She says we ought to call it 'The Ladies of the Blessed Sacrament."

Alice whooped musically into the telephone.

"And, Alice, listen! She says she'll work it up herself among the girls, the same as that Albert Corcoran among the boys."

"I didn't think she'd be so pious," Alice remarked, with that frankness so often associated with tender years.

"Neither did I," answered the dearest friend; "and I really don't know what to make of it."

The fact of the matter was that Miss Catherine Reno had lost considerable prestige since her late severe but short-lived headache. One member of the class had asked her whether the prospect of oranges could bring on a headache and then cure it. Others had made equally unfeeling remarks. But the boys on the street Were worse. They were always asking her about her precious health. And when doing so they were far too elaborate in their manner. Catherine, therefore, bearing these taunts meekly, was eagerly desirous to rehabilitat" herself. And now that the opportunity was thrust upon her she embraced it.

Within ten days both promoters had finished their work; and both presented them-selves to their respective directors. The Eucharistic Section and the Ladies of the Blessed Sacrament were adopted with enthusiasm, and the two Sodalities became in consequence more powerful for good than ever.

It must be confessed that there were few daily communicants on Pioneer Street. Alice and her dearest friend agreed to go six times a week. But to get up early Saturday morning! That was asking too much.

To the admiration of all that knew her, Catherine Reno was the shining exception. She arose on Saturday at six o'clock. The children of the square decided, in the language of Alice O'Shea, that Catherine was "dreadfully pious." Johnny O'Brien, however, had his doubts.

"Is she doing penance for playing possum?" he asked himself, "or is she really pious? Anyhow, it's a clear case of conversion."

But the model child, who, the tradition says, devoured eleven oranges at one sitting, giving the twelfth to her sister, kept her own counsel. Even to this day wild horses can not drag from her any further information concerning her "side-splitting" headache.

CHAPTER VIII

In which the author takes pleasure in introducing the Xaverian Acolytes engaged in se» cret service.

Y the way, Brother Crellin, did you hear of the latest from the Children of Mary?" asked Charles Bryan.

The two were in the acolytes' sacristy. Evening devotions for the first Friday in December were just over. The speaker, Charles Bryan, was the oldest member of the Xaverian Acolytes, a society lately organized by Brother Crellin and in its first fervor. It was made up of picked young men of St. Xavier Parish. They were, all of them, breadwinners, the youngest being eighteen years of age. It was their delight, besides serving the regular Masses when called upon, to take part in the more solemn ecclesiastical services. Charles Bryan, nearly thirty years of age, was one of the model young men of the Sixth Street Hill. Like Longfellow's blacksmith, he looked the whole world in the face, for he feared not any man. He was at once kind and brave. He had no human respect; and he was deeply religious. Every morning he served the half-

past-five o'clock Mass at the main altar. There were twenty-one members in the Junior Aco-lythical; and they were all clean-living, eager, earnest young men.

"No. Have they started a new section?"

"They wanted to; but they've got Father Carney so puzzled that he doesn't quite know what to do."

"For that matter," observed the Brother Sacristan, "they've had him on the run ever since Catherine Reno started the Communion Section. You see, Father Carney made her an officer at once, the Grand Secretary of the Ladies of the Blessed Sacrament; and so the idea spread among the Children of Mary that everybody who got up a new section would step right into office, and no questions asked. Within a week six different girls came to him, each with a section thought up out of her own head. One of them proposed a section the members of which should dress in black for the souls in purgatory ; a girl from the fifth grade brought in a fist of twenty from her class who declared themselves willing to visit public charitable institutions, including the jail and the workhouse. Poor Father Carney had no end of trouble in trying to combine in one act squelching and encouraging them."

Charles laughed.

"Well, it's the fifth grade again. Those little girls of ten and eleven are, with scarcely an exception, little angels. And I happen to know that several of them don't get their angelic qualities from home either. It's the school; it's the Sisters. Many of them are good in spite of their home life. Anyhow, I happened to call in to see Father Carney the day before yesterday on my way home from work. He was seated before his desk with a sheet of paper before him, and rubbing his cheek with his hand.

* 'Look at this, Charlie,' he said, handing me the paper. I glanced over the page. It had simply the names of forty-three girls. I asked him what it was; and he told me that they were the names of forty-three out of the fifty-one girls of the fifth grade, and that it was intended by the promoter, Miss Elizabeth Marie Lynam, to be the nucleus of a vocation section."

"What's that?" cried the sacristan, drawing a deep breath.

"A vocation section! Every girl on that list put her name down to be a nun!"

The Brother giggled.

"I laughed just the same as you did, Brother, when Father Carney told me what it meant. But he brought me up with a jerk.

88 HIS LUCKIEST YEAR

'It's no laughing matter,' said he. 'Just look closely at that list. I know every girl on it. Out of the forty-three signers there are ten who would sign anything. That leaves thirty-three. Well, out of those thirty-three there are four, or at most six, who under no conceivable conditions could embrace the religious life. That leaves twenty-seven.' Think of it, Brother Crellin! Twenty-seven pure young hearts turning so sweetly, so innocently to God! Every one of them has the makings of a spouse of Christ. Just now they are fragrant, tender flowers in the garden of God."

"So," put in Brother Crellin, "he's going to start a vocation section?"

"No; he's not."

"Why not?"

"He says he intends to spend a year or two longer in St. Xavier's. He's afraid of their parents."

"Oh, go on! He's not afraid."

"I don't think he is myself; but he said he's afraid of his life of angry mothers. And besides, he said that such a section might savor of novelty. He also said that, looking at that list of innocents, and thinking of what most of them would be in six years or so, it brought the tears to his eyes."

"I think I know how he feels," said the

Brother. "He's had the school now for over fourteen years; and he knows."

"I think I understand it myself, Brother. These little girls in the fifth grade are, most of them, pure as angels. Their hearts turn to God naturally. The church, the school, the Sisters who teach them, offset the dangers of the world. They are little angels. But just as soon as they are fourteen or fifteen out they go to work. Most of 'em don't have to go to work, but their parents want the extra money; and so out they go into the world before their character is formed, and in six months their vocation, if they ever had any, is killed."

"That's so," said the Brother. "A girl at fifteen is no longer a child, and not yet a woman. She lacks the safeguards of both, and is at the dangerous age."

"It's simply shocking to see how quickly they change," continued Charles. "They were sensible at eleven; at sixteen they are absolute geese. They paint and fix themselves up in a way that shows they have the taste of a Hottentot."

"Oh, I say, Charles; you're too hard on them. There are plenty of them who don't turn out that way at all."

"Oh, I wasn't talking of the Sodality girls

—not of those who stick to the Sodality when they go to work. No girl can have real devotion to the Blessed Virgin and live like a fool. The Sodalists are all right. It's those who leave school and Sodality both."

"I wonder what their parents—especially their mothers—are thinking of," said the Brother. "They ought to know what the Sodality means to their children. Why, in this down-town district it means everything/'

"If they don't know that," said Charles, "it's because they haven't enough sense to come in out of the rain when it's raining."

"I've been in other parishes," continued the Brother, looking through his glasses upon some invisible audience, "where the young men and the young women are either good or fairly good. But here it's different. They're either very good or downright bad."

"That's about it."

"In a place like this," continued the Brother, "where our young people are within a stone's throw of every indecent show-house and of the worst class of pool-rooms and of everything that leads to the primrose way, they've got to be mighty careful. If they are, they are leading strong and saintly lives. But if they are not careful, they become as pagan almost as their surroundings. And that's the reason our parish is made up of saints and sinners."

"It's enough to discourage Father Carney, isn't it, Brother?"

"No, Charles. He's not discouraged at all. He holds this: The growing children around here are exposed to dreadful temptations. Also, a number of them have careless or ignorant parents. Lots of them really do not seem to have a fair chance. Well, God, he holds, takes all that into account. They haven't the chance of the average Christian. They have poverty, and the danger of drink, and the danger of bad company, and no end of temptations. God fails to give them many things; but He makes it up by giving them one thing—a gift they received at the baptismal font, a gift cultivated in their Catholic training at school; and so when they've lost everything else that gift remains, and will in the end most probably save their souls."

"What gift is that, Brother?"

"The gift that the world laughs at and despises—the gift of Catholic faith. At the last, faith means everything, provided only they get the chance of repentance. And God is good. He will give it to them."

Charles was about to continue the conversa-
tion, when Bob Ryan suddenly entered, deep perplexity upon his face.

"Halloa, Bob," said Charles, "where have you left your smile? At the dry cleaner's?"

Charles and Bob, serving in the church at the same hour every morning, were already fast friends.

"Good evening, Brother. Halloa, Charlie; I didn't expect to find you here; but I'm mighty glad you are, because I want your advice, too, as well as Brother Crellin's. I'm in a peck of trouble."

"You are!" from both.

"Yes, I am. You know Angelo Corcoran?"

"He's a Xaverian Acolyte!" said Charles, in a manner which indicated that nothing more in the way of encomium need be said.

"Well, since his father's death he's been supporting the whole family. He's getting sixty a month."

"As nice a family as there is in our parish," commented the Brother.

"Don't I know it?" cried Bob. "I feel just as though I belonged to that family. Albert and I are partners, we study and read together. And Mrs. Corcoran is so good to me, always thinking up some kindness for me. She's "

"But what about Angelo?" interrupted the Brother.

"Oh, he's been burning the candle at both ends. He's been killing himself with work and study; and now he's on the verge of a breakdown."

Charles Bryan and Brother Crellin became as grave as Bob.

"Does that mean he'll have to stop work?" asked the Brother.

"It means that he'll drag along a little longer," returned Bob, "three or four or five weeks, and then collapse; or it means that if he stops right now and takes the proper treatment for about ten weeks he'll be all right."

"Who told you that?" asked the Brother.

"Young Doctor Keane. He's a great friend of mine. I got to know him through one of our sick boys he was attending. The doctor wants him to go to a hospital for ten weeks and he'll take care of him free."

"Fine," said Charles. "That settles it."

"I wish it did; but it doesn't," returned Bob.

"We can get him into a ward at the Good Samaritan, I think," argued Charles.

"Oh, that part's all right, too. I've seen Sister Regina myself, and she says she'll give him a special room, all to himself, and the best of nursing and care."

"Well, then, I should say that settles it," said Charles.

"No, it doesn't, Charlie. Sister Regina, when I began to thank her, stopped me short. She said I needn't thank her, because a kind woman, with a sad, sweet face—those were her words—from Hamilton had visited her a few weeks ago, and told her that if any deserving poor boy needed a room and care at the hospital the Sister might take him, and she would foot the bill."

"Well, I declare," said the Brother.

"Do you know her, Brother?" asked Charles.

"I suspect I do, Charles. There's a woman dressed in black—

"That's right," interrupted Bob, "she's in mourning. I remember the Sister said so."

"And she has the saddest and sweetest of faces," continued the Brother. "She comes to our church every month or so, and she always gives me ten dollars to spend on clothes and shoes for any poor altar boys. I know she doesn't belong to Cincinnati."

"I hope," said Bob fervently, "that I'll see her some day. But," he went on, "I'm still in a hole and can't see how I'm to climb out. Do you think Angelo would stop work and lie down for ten weeks, with his mother and brother and three sisters dependent upon him ?

I should say not! He's too game. And besides, he hasn't the least idea that he's on the brink of a breakdown. He feels sure that he'll be all right in a few weeks."

All three became silent.

"Couldn't Father Reardon persuade him to go?" asked Charles presently.

"Maybe he could," answered Bob; "but even if he did, that wouldn't settle the matter."

"Of course it wouldn't," put in Brother Crellin promptly. "In the meantime what's to become of the family? They can't live on air."

"That's just it, Brother," said Bob. "I happen to know that they're just out of debt at last. It was only three days ago that Mrs. Corcoran paid all the bills due since her husband's death; and she was so happy about it. She said that for the first time in ever so long she could breathe freely. But in paying those debts she put out every cent they had. If Angelo were to stop working next Saturday she would have to carry her family for ten weeks on fifteen dollars."

"But couldn't Mrs. Corcoran get some work?" asked Charlie. "She's young and active, and is a wonderful cook, and she can use a needle handily."

"Who's going to take care of the home and the children?" objected Bob.

"I don't like that scheme, Charlie," said Brother Crellin. "As the old song says, 'What is home without a mother.' From what I've noticed in this parish, I feel free to say that a lot of children, with their mothers working out by the day, are worse off than if they were in an orphan asylum. Of course, Mrs. Corcoran could do some sewing at home, and help out that way; but, first of all, the money she earned wouldn't be near enough, even if she got plenty of work; and, secondly, I doubt whether she'd get enough just now to keep her going as much as two hours a day."

"If we could only put Angelo in the hospital for ten weeks and keep his salary going on just the same," said Bob, his chin cupped in his right hand and his left supporting the elbow, "there would be no trouble at all. Gee! I wish I were rich; I'd pay it myself. Yesterday I got a letter from my friend Tom Temple. He sent me a check for thirty dollars, and told me to use it buying Christmas presents for my friends. I'm sure he wouldn't mind my using it for Angelo; but that would pay for just two weeks."

Charlie and Brother Crellin exchanged glances of wonder, which Bob, chin in hand and deeply absorbed, failed to perceive.

"That gives me an idea," Brother Crellin presently observed. "Most of our people are poor; but, according to their means, there are no more generous people in the country. Take, for instance, those young ladies of the Sodality. They are charitable to a fault. If Father Carney calls up fifteen of them, and tells them about the Corcoran family case, and asks each to contribute one dollar a week for ten weeks "

Brother Crellin left his sentence unfinished, in obedience to a protesting gesture from Charlie Bryan.

"No, you don't, Brother," cried Charlie, hi? face lighted up with animation. "The young ladies are all right; but we mustn't throw everything on them. Angelo is a Xaverian Acolyte. Why can't the Xaverian Acolytes take this thing up and see it through?"

"And leave me out!" exclaimed Bob rue* fully.

"We'll count you in as an honorary member, Bob; but we can get together fifteen dollars a week, I think."

"Hold on," interrupted Brother Crellin, looking both gratified and troubled. "We're not professional charity workers; we're not ranged under the banner of a 'statistical Christ.' "

"What's that?" asked Bob.

"How?" queried Charlie.

"It's possible," continued the Brother, "to be charitable and humane at the same time. Many charity workers don't know that; but it's so. Would it be the right thing, boys, for everybody in the parish to know that Mrs. Corcoran, who is a woman with self-respect, and her family are objects of public charity?"

"I should say notl" declared Bob emphatically.

"Of course," said Charlie, "we could keep it quiet among the boys."

"Twenty-one in number," stated the Brother Sacristan. "That's far too many. Besides, several of them are almost the sole support of their own mothers, and several are drawing very low salaries."

"That's so," assented Charlie. "And besides, there might be two or three who couldn't keep a secret."

Charlie paused for a moment, then added: "Oh, I've got it! We'll pick out six of them besides myself, and put them under secrecy. I can pick six that are absolute clams when it comes to keeping a secret. Then we'll each chip in two dollars a week, and Bob one dol-

lar; that makes fifteen. I'm sure with a little sacrifice we can all keep that up for ten weeks."

"That isn't fair," protested Bob. "One dollar! Why, I've thirty dollars. Put me down for three."

Meanwhile Brother Crellin had been going over the membership list of the Xaverian Acolytes.

"Let's make this a close corporation," he suggested. "The fewer in it, the less chance of its getting out. We'll make it six Xaverian Acolytes instead of seven. I see five on this list besides yourself, Charlie, who can spare the money and hold their tongues. Each will give two dollars a week, and Bob three."

"That's the stuff!" cried Bob radiantly.

Brother Crellin was an adept in the use of the telephone. Within twenty minutes the chosen acolytes were in the boys' sacristy. Then Brother Crellin set the matter before them.

"It's a privilege to come in on this," said John Reenan, the youngest of the Xaverians. "You can put me down. And I'll not even tell my mother."

"As for me," said William Denny, "it won't be hard at all. I was thinking of cutting cigars and tobacco out during Advent, and now

it's settled. That will save me one dollar a week, and I can easily afford the other."

In like manner spoke all.

"First rate!" said Charlie Bryan. "I guess we've got it all settled now."

"Oh, Lord!" cried Bob, who had been silent and thoughtful for several minutes. "It isn't settled at all."

"What's the matter?" cried several.

"Why, this. How are we going to get An-gelo to take the fifteen a week from us? He won't do it. And even if he were willing, what about his mother? She's never accepted charity in her life."

"That's a fact," said Will Denny. "And it would be rubbing it in on her in a way if she were to know that the people helping her were boys of the parish, some of whom she used to help herself. I don't mind saying that I was a mighty poor boy when I went to St. Xavier School; and she knew it, and she was always on the lookout for me when I passed her house. She always took me in and fed me — and sometimes I was mighty hungry. And more than once when my feet were on the ground"—here there was a slight break in the young man's voice— "she slipped me a pair of shoes. And I'll tell you something else, boys." Denny paused and held up an impressive hand.

"I'm willing to bet all my chances in life that she never told a soul what she did for me."

"That," said Brother Crellin, "is the charity of Christ."

Then up spoke in turn each of the Xaverian Acolytes. Two of them, like Denny, had been very poor boys, and these two had been helped by the good woman. All of them, at one time or another, had been fed.

"I had no idea," commented the Brother, "that Mrs. Corcoran, good as I knew her to be, was so charitable. In fact, it never occurred to me that she was able to do much in that line. She had a large family and very little money."

"Where there's a will there's a way," said Charlie.

"Anyway," pursued Brother Crellin, "we must imitate her in not letting the left hand know what the right hand's doing. And I've got an idea."

"Pass it around, Brother," said John Reenan.

"It's this. Father Carney is a great friend of Mrs. Corcoran's. She will stand for anything from him. Now, if he goes to her and tells her that he has arranged everything, and that Angelo is to go to the hospital for ten

weeks, and that he himself will bring her Angelo's salary each week, she'll obey him."

"Fine!" cried Bob.

"But she'll get suspicious," objected Charlie. "She'll want to know how the firm got to be so generous. In fact, she may ask who's paying the salary."

"I know it," asserted the Brother. "And all Father Carney has to do is to look severe and say that he's very much hurt at her asking any questions, and that he must insist on her doing just what he tells her. That wouldn't stop Mrs. Corcoran in dealing with most people; but in Father Carney's case it will."

Presently the delegation, headed by Brother Crellin, waited upon Father Carney. He listened without interruption.

"I declare!" he said. "Did you ever!" he added. "Boys, it's splendid. I'm proud I've had you at St. Xavier School. It seems to me I'm getting my reward in this world. You may go to bed to-night and sleep sound. I'll fix Mrs. Corcoran. If she starts to ask questions I'll take up my hat and look pained, and start to leave, and she'll give in for fear of hurting my feelings. My! but I'm glad that you show the true charity of Our Lord— for that's the kind of charity yours is. But I'm still gladder, in a way, that you're showing gratitude. It's a rare thing nowadays."

"Most of us," said Brother Crellin, "are grateful enough to people we expect to get something more out of."

"Oh, yes!" assented the priest. "But there's one thing I want to criticize."

"What's that, Father?" came the chorus.

"This thing concerns the Xaverian Acolytes. All the members ought to come in on it."

Eight people began to explain at once.

"Hold on, hold on!" cried the father. "You've explained that all to me already. Of course the whole thing is to be kept a dead secret. And I know it will be kept. But the other fifteen members ought to do something. Let them be formed into a flower committee and see that Angelo gets flowers twice a week."

And so it was settled out of hand.

As the young men left they each shook hands with Bob and thanked him as though he had done them a personal favor.

And, unusual as it may seem, everything was carried out according to the proposed arrangements. Angelo at the end of the week drew his salary; obtained, to his great delight, leave of absence for ten weeks; and, accompanied by Bob, went to the Good Samaritan Hospital for a stay of two months and a half.

CHAPTER IX

Narrating how Bob became prefect, the mystery of the Lady in Black, and the wonderful oration of Johnny O'Brien.

BOB was a popular boy in St. Xavier School, His kindness, his smile, his courtesy, won the good opinion of the girls, while his strength and skill in athletics made him the hero of the boys. Bob never quarreled. It was impossible to tease him. Jibes and jests and insinuations fell powerless before the armor of his good nature.

At Christmas time his popularity reached its acme. It came about in the following way: Anita sent him a Christmas box with enough cake, candy, nuts, raisins, and pie to last him a month. Mine host and hostess of the Blue Bird Inn, Mr. and Mrs. Symmes, enriched his larder with a number of turkeys and other eatables that would have made a feast for Lucullus. Tom Temple and Matt Morris sent him boxes, too; while the venerable Mose and his ancient wife remembered him in the shape of the famous blanket he had once worn in their modest hut.

Bob, seeing that he was heavily over-supplied, went to Father Carney and obtained permission to have the use of the St. Xavier tea-room. He gave the St. Aloysius Sodality a banquet. There were one hundred and twenty invitations, and one hundred and nineteen acceptances. The one hundred and twentieth boy was down with tonsilitis; and, the story goes, it took the united efforts of his mother, one strong brother, and three sisters to hold him down in his bed when the banquet hour drew nigh.

Mrs. Corcoran, bright and alert as ever, took charge of the kitchen. She declared, an hour before the guests seated themselves, that she had provisions enough for two hundred. An hour later she had her doubts. The youthful banqueters did not seem to share her opinion. One loaf of bread, overlooked in a hidden corner of the pantry, was the only bit of perishable goods left when the happy guests arose and gave three cheers for Bob and three for the good lady and her assistants.

"I think," observed Johnny O'Brien, as the boys made their way downstairs, "that Bob Ryan would be a fine prefect for our Sodality."

Judging by the effect produced, this was the happiest remark that ever dropped from Johnny's eloquent tongue.

The duly elected prefect had left school just before the holidays to go to work, and by doing so had automatically ceased to be a member of the St. Aloysius Sodality. So there was more than academic suggestion in Johnny's remark.

One week later the officers were summoned to nominate three names for the prefectship. Bob got every vote but his own. The members, following the lead of the officers, then elected Bob to the prefectship, by the handsomest majority ever given in any boys' Sodality of Cincinnati.

Bob inaugurated his term in office by introducing an athletic section. The sessions were held on Friday and Saturday nights in the schoolboys' playroom. At the suggestion of Charlie Bryan he started the boys with boxing and wrestling.

"You see, it's this way," Charlie explained. "Nearly every boy with good red blood in him, like—like — well, like us Irish, is more or less pugnacious. And the trouble is they haven't much chance for a real, good, honest fight. Generally speaking, there's always something wrong about fighting, and half the fights that do come off among the boys come from the fact that one boy is just naturally dead curious to find out whether he isn't stronger than some other boy."

"I guess that's so," said the new prefect.

"Well, they'll have their very natural curiosity gratified with boxing and wrestling or with both, and then there's something else; they'll learn the great lesson of self-restraint."

"How's that, Charlie?"

"Why, we will teach them to keep their tempers. As soon as a boy gets mad we'll call him to order. If he doesn't correct himself, we'll take him out and put another boy in his place. You'll do the teaching, Bob, because you know more about it than any of our fellows; but I'll be on hand with some of the other Xaverian Acolytes to act as referees."

"George!" exclaimed Bob, "that will be great. And you'll tell them they must keep their tempers?"

"Oh, no," answered Charlie. "Some of them might think we were mixing the thing up with a Sunday-school class. We'll tell them to keep cool, to be game."

"I see," said Bob grinning. "As Johnny O'Brien would put it, they must all be good sports."

"Exactly."

With the successful inauguration of boxing and wrestling, tempered by dumb-bell and Indian club exercises, the fighting spirit of the

youth attending St. Xavier's found a sufficient outlet. They all became Johnny O'Briens.

Bob was now busier than ever. His studies, his duties as prefect, his visits as member of the Sick Committee, to which committee William Devine and Edward Bolan were now added, and his task as athletic instructor gave him little or no free time. He was too busy to worry; too busy to give thought to the mystery that might else have clouded his life; too busy to realize that he was alone in the world, and that by the end of the school year his money would be exhausted and he would be unprovided for.

Toward the end of February Bob was seated beside Angelo in a bright room in the Good Samaritan Hospital.

"Well, Angelo, how do you feel?"

"I feel, I feel—I feel like a morning star. I've been here nine weeks, Bob. There's just one more left. But, goodness gracious me! I've been well for the last ten days—never felt so well in all my life. I wanted to go out last week; but Dr. Keane said nix."

"I guess he knows best," said Bob. "He's awfully proud of your case. He told me so himself; and he says that if you take just common care of yourself you'll be better now than you ever were in your life."

"That's the way I feel. And, Bob, I got a mighty nice letter from my firm. They say that they've learned in my absence how much work I've been doing, and that my place is open to me, even if I need to stay away for six months or a year."

"That's some compliment," said Bob.

"I guess it's because I'm quick at figuring, Bob. I got that from my father. When I leave here next week I'm going to give up extra lessons and studies."

"The doctor says you must!' said Bob. "He sa^s; you can take up the extras when you're nineteen or twenty* Say, what beautiful flowers you've got!"

"**Aren't ihey? They've been coming every day, •Bob, besides the flowers from the Xaver-ian Acolytes. For a long time I wondered who was sending them. Now I think I know."

"You do? I've been wondering, too. Lots of boys have been trying to find out. Who is it?"

"You remember me telling you about the very nice quiet lady who came to see me the first week I was here?"

"The one who didn't give any name who left you a basket of fruit?"

"That's the one. She was here again yesterday. And she brought me more fruit; and,

though her face is very sad, she smiles so sweetly and seemed to feel so very glad because I was so much better."

As Angelo spoke, Bob's eyes widened and a great wonderment showed upon his features. He cupped his chin in his familiar pose.

"When I thinl of her," Angelo continued, "I always think of her as the Lady in Black."

Bob jumped to his feet.

"The Lady in Black!" he repeated.

"Yes; she's dressed in mourning. She has the gentlest face I ever saw. But there's something strange about her f°re, too, that puzzled me. The Sister in charge of this floor says that she must have suffered a good deal, and the nurse says that it must be the loss of her husband."

"Does she live in Hamilton?" asked Bob.

"Why, Bob Ryan, who tokl you about her?"

"She's fond of boys, isn't she, Angelo?"

"You talk as if you knew her, Bob. The nurse says that she comes here about once a month and visits all the sick children, especially the boys. Anyhow, I'm now almost dead certain that she's the one who has been sending me flowers every day."

"I wish I did know her," said Bob, seating himself once more, and putting his hand under his chin.

"And she wishes that she knew you, Bob."

"What!"

"Just as I said. I was telling her about your Sodality and your Sick Committee and your being prefect and your athletic section, and she was so pleased—no, that's too weak a word—she was so delighted! What took her most was your care of the sick. She says she hopes to meet you some day."

"I hope she will, Angelo," said Bob fervently.

"By the way," Angelo began, after a short pause, "has your Sodality anything new on hand?"

"I should say we have. We're going good, as Johnny O'Brien says, but we want to go better. The gym class is full, and the boys are learning to take hard knocks without losing their tempers. The Communion Section, the Brothers tell me, has produced wonderful results. But we're springing a new move for this Lent."

"What's that?"

"It isn't anything original, Angelo; it's just trying to do in a small way what the Young Ladies' Sodality have been doing for years. You know, during Lent we all make some little sacrifices. A lot of the boys cut out moving pictures, and no end of them stop eating

112 HIS LUCKIEST YEAR

candy. Now, what we propose to do is to get the kids to put aside the money they would else spend for candy and moving pictures and things like that, and hand it over to Father Reardon for a fund to go to the Jesuit mission in British Honduras."

"Why the British Honduras mission, Bob?"

"Oh, we've had a lecture on it from a former missionary there, and he told us they needed money badly just now; and besides, the fellows know some of the men who were missionaries there; and so we thought it might interest them more than if we worked for the foreign missions in general."

"Do you think the boys will take to it, Bob?"

"I hope so; but I'm not so sure. We announced it two weeks ago, and we started the collection last Sunday. The first Sunday of Lent only six boys reported, and the amount turned in was fifty-seven cents."

"That's not so very bad, Bob."

"I don't know. I put in twenty-five cents myself. At the rate we're going we'll get about three dollars. The kids are all right; but sometimes you've got to club them almost to wake them up. I wish I knew how I could get them interested."

Bob had some cause to worry in regard to this, his pet scheme. On the following Sunday eleven boys reported, their self-denial offerings coming to eighty-one cents. It was discouraging. Then—to be precise, on the following Tuesday—something happened.

It was half-past three in the afternoon, the time for the dismissal of the classes. Bob Ryan, who was to stay for special work in the eighth grade, came hurrying into the yard to deliver a note from his teacher to a boy of a lower grade. He caught the boy at the gate and, having handed him the note, was about to return, when Alice O'Shea came running up to him, holding in her hand a cheap-looking publication.

"Listen, Bob," she cried. "There's a man standing over at our gate; and he's giving a copy of this to each little girl as they come out."

Bob took the paper and glanced over its headlines.

There is a species of publication, quite common in the backwoods of America, which has its reason for existing founded on the gospel of hate. Under the name of patriotism—that patriotism, by the way, which has been aptly defined as "the last refuge of a scoundrel"— it attacks Catholics, their doctrines, their practices, their priests, the nuns. Every issue of such papers is well seasoned with lubricity,

which has an appeal to a large circle of readers; every issue abounds in the truth which is half a truth, and consequently worse than a lie ; every issue smacks of listening at keyholes and of backstairs gossip. These papers pretend to represent patriotism and Protestantism. They are an infamous libel on both.

Such a paper was the one in Bob's hand. We shall call it the Unspeakable. For the second time in the recorded history of Bob Ryan his face flushed with anger. He tore the paper to pieces, and threw it into a waste-paper box placed near the boys' gate.

"Here, fellows," he cried to two of the fifth-grade boys, "get hold of this waste-paper box, and bring it over as quick as you can to the girls' side."

Then Bob, followed by the eager-eyed Alice, hastened to the sidewalk, and paused for a moment to see what was being done.

A nondescript fellow of about thirty years of age, with a beard of several days' growth, was handing the little girls of the lower grade, as they issued from the school grounds, a copy of the Unspeakable.

"Take that home to your mother," he said from time to time.

Bob drew nearer, followed almost immediately by the two willing boys of the fifth grade with their waste-paper box, provided graciously by a municipality to help keep the city clean.

"Alice," he said, "round up all those little girls who have gone off with those papers, and tell them to bring them back to me."

At the words, Alice with speeding feet hastened to obey.

Then Bob halted the two girls who had just received copies of the fragrant sheet.

"Hand 'em here, children," he said, with his old smile. "Your mother wouldn't want that thing in her house."

"Take 'em, Bob," said one, handing her copy to him as though she were receiving a favor.

The second girl made a like speech.

He tore the two copies into bits, and threw them into the municipal can.

The agent of the Unspeakable forgot his work, and fixed upon Bob eyes of anger. He might as well not have fixed them, however, so far as the boy was concerned. Bob was too intent upon the matter in hand to take any interest in facial expression.

"Here, Bob, take mine"- "Take mine, Bob."- -"I was here first; take mine."

For Bob was surrounded now by the sweet, innocent children of the first grade, all clamor-

ing in tiny accents to be relieved of the Unspeakable.

Bob, for the next three or four minutes, was the busiest boy in Cincinnati; the man, the most glaring. Between Bob and himself was a host of little girls, all trying to reach Bob, not one of them conscious of the awful glare.

"I'm with you, Bob," cried a familiar voice, "pass 'em to me, and I'll help tear 'em up."

It was that prince of sports, Johnny O'Brien.

There were others with him presently, boys from the fifth and sixth grades. The can was fast filling with Unspeakable*. Meanwhile, the girls of the third grade caught the idea, and proceeded each to tear up her own particular copy. Very shortly the crowd about Bob thinned; and the man, ceasing to glare, had recourse to action.

Advancing to Bob, he held a paper toward him.

"Do you want this paper, sonny?"

"Yes," answered Bob, "I'll take all you give me."

"Now," said the agent of the Unspeakable, handing Bob a copy, "I'd like to see you tear that up."

"Then you'll see it, all right," said Johnny O'Brien,

And so he did.

Without further word the enraged fellow gave Bob a sound smack on the cheek.

"Take that, will you?" he added.

The man, very properly, regarded Bob as a boy. And so he looked. Bob was dressed like any other lad of fourteen years.

Bob raised his head and looked surprised. It may seem remarkable, but the fact is that he showed no sign of anger. Not for nothing had he conducted the gym classes.

Then a brilliant idea occurred to the aggressor. He would humiliate that impudent boy before the whole crowd. Reaching forward an incautious hand to catch Bob by the nose, the man suddenly saw stars and felt the pavement. For Bob's good right hand had shot out and caught the aggressor right at the point of the chin.

With ill-suppressed curses the fellow arose, and, instead of renewing the attack, put his right hand into his hip pocket.

"Quick, Bob," cried Johnny O'Brien, "he's got a gun."

Bob did not need this admonition. As the hand moved to the pocket Bob struck out once more, and once more the man went down with a precipitancy which must have been hard on the concrete sidewalk.

The fellow, somewhat dazed but still sufficiently conscious, sat up, making no attempt to rise, and, fixing eyes of malignity upon the boy, once more reached for his hip pocket. With the quickness of a trained wrestler in perfect condition, Bob was upon him and pinned him to the sidewalk.

"Quick!" he cried, "get Jerry."

"He's coming, he's coming!" piped a chorus of voices.

Through the crowd of children came the janitor of St. Xavier's.

"Here, let me at him," he cried.

"Look out, Jerry," said Johnny O'Brien. "He's got a gun in his pocket."

"He'll not have it long," said Jerry, pushing Bob aside and beginning his experiments on the agent of the Unspeakable by knocking him flat.

Then Jerry took the man by the feet and held him up on high. Out from his pockets fell: one pistol, one vicious-looking knife, a blackjack, several pieces of silver, and a lot of pictures and leaflets, all of them a trifle more unspeakable than the unspeakable paper itself.

"You let go of me," shouted the man, restored to his feet, trembling with rage and fear.

Jerry reversed him once more, and was thus holding him when Officer Brierly laid a hand upon the janitor.

"What's the charge, Jerry?"

"Oh, there's no charge at all. I'm willing to give him another shaking, free, too."

"But what has he done?"

Jerry calmly restored the man to his feet.

"He's carrying a pistol; and look at the dirty stuff I shook out of his pockets. And he's been passing a dirty paper out to the little girls of this school."

The officer put his arm about the terror-stricken man.

"I'll take him, Jerry: we'll have several charges against him."

"Sure, you're welcome to him. He's too small for me. Say, officer, while we're waiting for the patrol would you mind my giving him a sound spanking?"

Brierly grinned.

"The patrol is coming," he said.

A few moments later Johnny O'Brien, mounted on the wooden box procured for the occasion, yelled at the top of his voice:

"Attention, you kiddies."

The children who had waited to see the patrol wagon take away the prisoner were in no hurry to leave. Johnny's face, alight with

120 HIS LUCKIEST YEAR

enthusiasm, drew them, one might say, magnetically.

"You saw Bob Ryan do up that bigoted short skate, didn't you?"

"Yes, Sister," answered most of the girls.

"Well, that's the kind of a poor fish our Catholic missioners have got to go up against. Those fellows are liars and cowards."

"Hurrah 1" cried Johnny O'Brien's sister.

"Hurrah!" echoed a hundred small boys.

The girls squealed approbation.

"Two weeks ago," continued Johnny, gesticulating wildly, "Bob Ryan started our Sodality to get up a fund —a lot of money, you know — to help our missioners. And is the money coming in? Not so as you can notice it. And look here, you kiddies. That fellow who's just gone off a joy-riding in the patrol wagon has handed out free more copies of his measly old paper than all the money we have collected could pay for. Ain't that nice?"

"Yes, Johnny," answered a little girl seriously.

Most of the girls nodded their heads in assent.

"Aw, go on home!" growled Johnny, and got down.

One hundred little girls followed the disgusted orator's advice. They went home, and with shining eyes and voluble tongues related all the incidents leading up to the arrest, concluding with Johnny O'Brien's flash of oration. These innocent children varied extremely in their several accounts. Nevertheless, three distinct and uniform impressions were firmly established throughout the parish:

1st. Bob Ryan knocked out a big man who hated the Catholic Church.

2nd. The man was trying to offset the good work of the British Honduras missionaries.

3rd. Bob Ryan was trying to get up a fund to help the missionaries against these bigots.

There was a general opinion, also, to the effect that Johnny O'Brien would go to Congress some day.

Next morning three little girls—two of them twins—brought Bob three dollars for his fund. In the afternoon eight innocents added four dollars more.

On the following day, there was so great a throng of donors that Bob was forced to get an assistant. The story spread. All the girls in the upper grades began to show interest. Nickles and dimes and quarters came rolling in. Last of all the St. Aloysius Sodality woke up. It was their work, and it was the girls

who were doing it. The spirit of generosity spread.

By the end of Lent, the amount subscribed to the British Honduras fund totaled seven hundred and twenty-five dollars.

CHAPTER X

In which the mystery concerning the late Mr. Corcoran is cleared, and Mrs. Corcoran learns much from Bob Ryan.

N a Saturday morning toward the close of Lent there was a knock at Bob's door.

"Come in," chirped Bob blithely. "Oh," he cried, jumping to his feet, "is it you, Mrs. Corcoran?"

"Good morning, Bob. I've come to have a talk with you."

Bob, smiling radiantly, moved the finest chair in his room from a corner.

"Sit down, Mrs. Corcoran. I had no idea it was you who knocked. I thought it was one of the boys."

"Now, look here, Bob Ryan; my boy, An-gelo, is well and working, and he's going to get a raise of ten dollars on the first of next month."

"By George!" cried Bob; "that's just bully."

"And all the ten weeks he was sick, and you visited him, he drew his fifteen dollars a week."

"That was fine!" said Bob.

"Now, Bob, where did that money come from?"

Bob turned rosy. He looked at Mrs. Corcoran, opened his mouth as though about to reply, but uttered no sound.

"Bob Ryan," she repeated, "where did that money come from?"

"Why don't you ask Father Carney?" he gasped.

"Bob Ryan, where did that money come from?"

"Why—where—Oh, Jiminy—what makes you ask?"

"Because," answered Mrs. Corcoran, "two days ago my boy got a letter from his firm, and in that letter it said that it wasn't their custom to pay salary to their office force when on the sick list, but that in view of certain corrections they had just discovered which my boy had made in their accounts a week before he went to the hospital, and which saved the firm several hundred dollars, they had resolved to make an exception in his case, and so they enclosed a check for seventy-five dollars—half pay for the ten weeks he was away."

"Yes," said Bob. "And do you know, Mrs. Corcoran, that Albert, my best friend, is the finest boy in the eighth grade?"

"We're not talking about Albert," rejoined Mrs. Corcoran.

"Have you ever taken a look at my room? There are some mighty nice pictures in it. Look here," and Bob arose, "this picture over my desk "

"Sit down, Bob Ryan; we're not talking about pictures."

"Oh, hang it!" blurted Bob. "We just knew you wouldn't stand for any charity. It was a trick."

"Bob Ryan, tell me about it."

Bob had a miserable quarter of an hour. He tried to suppress his own part; but Mrs. Corcoran's direct and pointed questions left him no loophole of escape. The whole story came out.

Then Mrs. Corcoran took out her handkerchief and wept.

"Oh, don't do that, ma'am. Please don't," pleaded Bob.

But she continued to weep.

"I—I—wouldn't hurt your feelings," Bob exclaimed, "for anything in the world. Oh, Mrs. Corcoran, we certainly meant all right."

Then Mrs. Corcoran, with the tears standing in her eyes, raised her face and smiled.

"Bob Ryan, God bless you," and she wiped her eyes. "And God bless Father Carney and

Brother Crellin and Charlie Bryan and all those boys. And what I say now I'm going to keep on saying as long as I'm able to pray."

"That's good of you," said Bob.

"We're as happy a home now as there is in Cincinnati. We want nothing; and if God continues to help us, we shall soon be able to help others."

"You're always helping others," said Bob.

"Bob, I'm going to tell you something which nobody but my confessor knows."

Bob grew alarmed once more.

"I married a very clever man and a good man, too. But from the second year of my marriage until his death I carried an awful burden. It lasted nearly twenty years, and I carried it alone. I tried to be brave; I tried to keep a smiling face. I tried to make both ends meet, with nothing at either end, and sometimes I got so desperate that I spent hours before the Blessed Sacrament. If it weren't for daily communion I think I'd have gone mad."

"What in the world was the matter?" thought Bob, but he said nothing.

"The fact is," continued Mrs. Corcoran, "my husband was a gambler."

"Oh!" cried Bob.

a scientific one. He was amazing at figures, as you know, and he had a hobby on the laws of chance."

"Oh!" cried Bob once more, beginning at last to see a light.

"From the first years of our marriage he took to figuring out how to beat the races. As a result, nearly all his salary was thrown away on his experiments. When I married him, I had three thousand dollars. The day you came to see Albert as the Sick Committee I had spent the last cent of that money."

"You must have had a hard time, Mrs. Corcoran."

"It was especially hard the last six months of my husband's life. He thought he had discovered at last a sure method of beating the races, and he worked at it night and day. He assured me that he'd soon be a millionaire. Sometimes I feared he was going insane. In the meantime I saw nothing but ruin and starvation ahead."

"Now I understand, ma'am," said the sympathetic boy.

"I don't know how I bore it the last four weeks of his life," continued the good woman. "I don't know how I kept the secret from my friends. Why, when he talked often about buying a house at Clifton and stopping work,

it was all I could do to keep from screaming. It was—it was—hard."

"I should say so," assented Bob.

"And then he quit work."

"I remember," said Bob.

"And the next day, Bob, he went over to stake his whole salary on the plan he had figured out —the plan which he said was sure to win. And when he was at the races I was kneeling before the Blessed Sacrament. I was there for three hours—the three blackest hours of my life."

"That was terrible," whispered Bob.

"Yes; but I thought even then how Our Lord suffered in the Garden of Gethsemane, and the thought made me brave. Then I got up and went out of the church and returned home. The news of my husband's death followed me into the house. And, Bob, while it was a shock, I could not but wonder whether it was an answer to my prayers. And when that good priest who was at my husband's side in his last hours came to me and brought his dying message, I knew it was an answer to prayer. Bob, my husband was himself in his last conscious moments; he was the man I married twenty years ago. He made a good confession; he was heartily sorry for a wasted life, and he told the priest that he had been a de-

luded fool. He sent his dearest love to me and the children; he begged my forgiveness, and he died from the shock that came from finding that all his studies and calculations for beating the races had come to nothing. Best of all, he died humbled, repentant, with the sacred name of Jesus upon his lips."

"Thank God for that, ma'am."

"I'm telling you this, Bob, because I trust you and love you as my own son. You were right, my boy; I fear I'd have been too proud to accept help even from Father Carney. But it was done. And my boy is saved. And want and poverty are no longer threatening; and my children are well and happy, and I am grateful beyond any words. As for those young men who helped, they are just noble. I'll never, never forget what you and they have done. Sometimes, Bob, I have seen some mighty mean and ugly things in human nature. Perhaps I shall meet such things again. But no matter how ugly they may be, I'll always think of Brother Crellin and Bob Ryan and Charlie Bryan, and I'll know that this world is worth while and that God created us a little lower than the angels."

"I know lots of mighty good people," said Bob. "This parish is just full of them. And on my road down here last summer I met the nicest people in the world. You see that picture of the little girl over my desk? That's Anita Reade. She's one of my best friends. I get a letter from her every week. Hasn't she a nice face. She's full of energy. The Reades are the nicest family I ever met."

"How did you come to meet them, Bob?'* "Well, you know, Mrs. Corcoran, all my trouble began last summer. I'd been living in Dubuque with my father and his old housekeeper, who brought me up. Pa was fond of money, but he didn't care much for me." "How about your mother, Bob?" "I never saw her. Pa says she died when I was a baby of six months. Well, anyhow, on July 5th of last year, my father took me off from Dubuque in a machine. We rode till it was very late at night. And then he ordered me to get down; he gave me fifty dollars and told me not to show my face in Dubuque for one year. He said I was to go South, and if I didn't do what he told me I'd be arrested. Then I met the nicest man you ever saw, the first thing next morning. His name is Tom Temple, and he's a poet, and he writes the nicest things in rhymes. He tramped with me down along the Mississippi river, and got me interested in books and poetry. We had

fine times, till we got caught in a thunderstorm and Tom Temple took a chill."

"And what did you do, Bob, when he got sick?"

"A jolly old man named Mose found us out in the storm, and he took us to his hut, where his wife was sitting on the bed, smoking a pipe. They gave us shelter for the night, and old Mose is the funniest old man I ever saw. He's over eighty, but he's as strong as an ox. When he was a man of forty-five he took a horse weighing over eleven hundred pounds, raised it completely off the ground and carried it seven feet. No other man from Davenport to Dubuque, the people say, was able to do that. And would you believe it, Mrs. Corcoran, my pa was right about the police being after me."

"Why, Bob, surely you never did anything wrong!"

"Not that I know of, ma'am. But the morning after I got to Mose's house there were two detectives came along looking for a man and a very fat boy. I was the fat boy, ma'am, but I've trained down. My partner, Tom Temple, was already in the hospital, but Mose didn't tell the detectives the truth. He sent them off on a wrong scent. I was hiding in the house, and they didn't come in."

"And did the detectives trouble you any more?"

"No, ma'am; that's the last I heard of them. But I was afraid they would catch Tom Temple. They told Mose that Tom had kidnaped the boy with him. Just think of a poet like Tom being a kidnaper. All the same, they managed to track him up to the hospital. He was delirious when they arrived, and so he didn't know anything about it at the time. He was up visiting there again about a month ago, and the nurse who had been waiting upon him told him how the two detectives came in and looked at him hard for five minutes, and took out their note-books and a photograph, and then said that he wasn't the man they were looking for at all, and that they had wasted their time running after the wrong pair."

"So they didn't want you at all, Bob?"

"That's what I would think; but Tom Temple's got a different idea. He says they were looking for me."

"That's strange, my boy."

"And Tom says I must try to get back to Dubuque next summer. He says there's a mystery about my case that ought to be cleared."

"So you hear from him, do you?"

"Every two weeks or so, Mrs. Corcoran. Well, after I left Mose and his wife I met the nicest man and woman you ever saw. They were the landlord of the Blue Bird Inn and his wife. They gave me a dinner fit for a king. The lady cooked it, and she's just the kind of cook you are. And she's nice and kind like you. Her husband was fat and jolly. They helped me buy a boat, and Mrs. Symmes "

"Who?" cried Mrs. Corcoran.

"The lady of the Blue Bird Inn."

"What name did you say?"

"Mrs. Symmes, ma'am."

"Mrs. John Symmes?"

"Why, how did you know her name? Here's her picture. She was as nice a woman as ever I met. Why, what's the matter, Mrs. Corcoran?"

The good woman had taken one quick glance at the photograph which Bob had selected from a number on his desk, and then sank back into her chair. Her eyes closed. Bob feared she had fainted.

The boy hastily procured a glass of water and put it to her lips. Mrs. Corcoran opened her eyes presently.

"Give me that picture, Bob."

Holding it in her hands, she gazed at it long and earnestly, then pressed it to her lips.

"No wonder I remind you of her, Bob; that's my youngest sister."

"Oh!" cried Bob. It was now his turn to sit down.

"Our family was broken up by death when I was quite young," went on Mrs. Corcoran. "And my little sister, who was then barely five, was taken by some relatives living in Indiana. After it was too late we learned that they were fallen-away Catholics. They did all they could to make the little one forget us. So, as the years went on, we almost lost complete track of her. I just learned by the merest accident a few months ago that she was married to a man named John Symmes. Oh, Bob, what a small world it is I Tell me all about her."

And then Bob became eloquent. Into his story entered the details of his buying The

Wanderer, that splendid boat, and of his receiving the best of dogs, Hobo.

"And when I bade her good-by," concluded Bob, "she—she kissed me."

"I don't blame her, Bob," said Mrs. Corcoran, "if she thought half as much of you as I do. And I'm so glad that she feels so nicely toward Catholics. She is baptized a Catholic, and probably doesn't know it. So you've got her address?"

"Yes, ma'am; and I'll write her a letter tonight and tell her about you."

"And I," rejoined Mrs. Corcoran, "will write her a letter to-night and tell her all about you. But what became of Hobo and the boat, Bob?"

"I'm telling you my whole story, ma'am. You've told me yours. Well, with that boat I began to make money. You see, I wanted to study for another year and finish the eighth grade. I sold fish, and hired my boat, and had a great time. And one day, going down the river, I met the Reades."

"Oh, Anita's people."

"Yes; they're the nicest family I ever met. Tom Reade goes to Campion College; he's a bird. And Lucille! She's just a lovely young lady—tall and stately. She and Tom were almost Catholics when I met them. I spent a day with them, and it was one of the happiest days of my life. They treated me as if I belonged to the family."

"Everybody does that to you, Bob."

"It was hard for me to leave them. A day or so afterward a rich man offered me a big price for my boat. So I sold it. That was hard, too. While I was wondering what to do next and sitting alone by the river bank, along came a boy named Matt Morris, in a

canoe ; and we became friends right away. He was living in the woods — he was a Campion boy, too — and he agreed to instruct me for first communion if I'd live with him. You see, my pa wouldn't bring me up a Catholic, though he let me know I was baptized."

"That's a funny father you had."

"He was queer," admitted Bob. "Of course, I was dead anxious to get ready for communion, and so I stayed with Matt Morris. He was a great athlete, and he put me through a course of stunts that took away most of my fat, and made me a good boxer and wrestler, and things of that kind. Oh, but we did have good times! We were happy as butterflies. And then, just as the three weeks were up, a thief got into our cave and stole a lot of stuff, along with my money. I caught him as he was running away and got him down and made him empty out everything he had stolen."

"Your boxing and wrestling came in handy, Bob."

"It surely did. All the same, if it hadn't been for my dog, Hobo, I think that thief might have killed me. He killed poor Hobo with one blow, and then I got mad and kicked him to the door of our place. And Matt fin-

ished what I began. I guess Matt was mad, too."

"It served him perfectly right," said Mrs. Corcoran.

"And then," Bob continued, "who should come along but Mr. Reade. Anita was very ill and was calling for me. Of course, I went, and that broke up our camp. But I'll never forget Matt Morris. He was one of the best friends I ever had."

"Are all your friends up North?"

"I should say not. Why, there's Albert. He's one of the best friends I ever had."

"And what about the people on this street?"

"Why, they're all friends of mine. There's little Alice O'Shea. She's always gay and smiling and in good humor. She has a heart as big as herself. And there's Johnny O'Brien, the sport of Pioneer Street. He's true as gold. And there's Alice's best friend, little Elizabeth Reno, with the bobbed hair and the quaint smile that wrinkles her nose. Why, I never had better friends than they."

Mrs. Corcoran broke into a ringing laugh.

"Look here, Bob Ryan. All your geese are swans. Do you know that whenever you talk about any of your friends you always say that each particular one is one of the best friends you ever had?"

"Is that so?" exclaimed Bob. "Why, I never noticed till you told me. That's funny, isn't it?"

"No, it isn't funny," corrected Mrs. Corcoran. "It's just beautiful. Well, you went to visit Anita?"

"Yes, and she wanted to be baptized a Catholic, and she got so ill that very night that I baptized her myself. And then we took her to the Good Samaritan Hospital here to see a famous children's specialist, and she got well. And Lucille and Tom became Catholics and went to communion with Anita at the hospital. While I was there I met Brother Cyril, and that settled me. I had found my teacher, and my school, and my grade."

"It was a good thing for all of us, Bob, when you came to stay."

"Look at this room," cried Bob, arising and waving his hands. "See how beautifully it's fixed up. Well, the Reades did that. My, but they were kind to me! You'd think I had done something wonderful for them; and I was just simply nice and friendly because I loved them."

"Don't you like everybody you meet, Bob?"

"Pretty much all of them, ma'am."

"And that's why everybody likes you. The boys of the Sodality swear by you. Anything you say goes. Father Carney has noticed the difference. You've put life into the Sodality; it's a going concern. And you've stopped a lot of fussing and fighting. Even in your class, Brother Cyril says, there's more fun and more hard work than he ever dreamed possible. Things are going better at the school than ever before in its long history."

"Well, you see, Mrs. Corcoran, with boys like your Albert, who is one of my very "

The good lady's laugh brought him to a pause.

"Oh, I beg your pardon. Anyhow, with boys like Albert and Will Devine and Edward Bolan and Johnny the dead-game sport, and a lot of others like them, it's no wonder that everything is going well. But," added Bob, after a pause, "there's one thing that worries me."

"What's that?"

"The girls on our street. About a week ago Lulu Jones got into a scrap with Marie Cramer. All the other girls took sides. And now one-half of the girls won't speak to the other half."

"That's the way with girls," commented the good woman. "They fall out easily, and they say they'll never speak to each other again, and the next day they're walking arm in arm."

"Yes; but this time it's different, Mrs. Corcoran. They don't make up, and a lot of them have stopped going to daily communion. Why, even Alice won't speak to her dearest friend on earth, Elizabeth Reno."

"Oh, is that so?" cried Mrs. Corcoran. "Then some of the parents have taken a hand in the row."

"That's a fact," assented Bob. "I remember now several mothers paid their respects to each other."

"Precisely. Some mothers love their children not wisely but too well.

"If the little girls were left to themselves," said Mrs. Corcoran, "they'd have their little fallings-out one minute and forget them the next."

"I never thought of that," said Bob. "I'm glad you told me. Maybe, now, I can fix it up."

And, if we may anticipate, on the following day Bob, who had read the life of St. Monica, the mother of St. Augustine, did actually bring about peace. He told the warring women all the nice things each had said of the other.

"And you hear from all these absent friends?" continued Mrs. Corcoran.

"I certainly do. Even from old Mose, who can neither read nor write. His wife, Anna, sends me letters. It keeps me busy keeping up with them; but it's worth while. And do you know, Mrs. Corcoran, there's one funny thing about these letters. In the beginning of the school year Tom Temple and Lucille in all their letters were always writing about each other. Tom's letters were all about Lucille, and Lucille's were all about Tom."

"That's clear," said Mrs. Corcoran, "they were in love."

"But, you see, they had never seen each other."

"Oh," said Mrs. Corcoran, "I suppose you wrote to Tom all you knew about Lucille, and you told Lucille all you knew about Tom."

"How did you guess that?"

"And on the strength of your talk and your letters it was a case of love before first sight."

"Do you think so? Well, maybe it was. Anyhow I told the truth. But here's the funny part. They met each other early in December; and since that time they don't say a word about each other in their letters."

"You don't say!" cried Mrs. Corcoran. "I guess, Bob, you spoke about them too flatteringly."

"I didn't," returned Bob stoutly. "I only told the truth. Lucille is the nicest young lady I ever met. She's one of my

142 HIS LUCKIEST YEAR

A ringing laugh put an end to Bob's panegyric of the "tall and stately" Lucille.

"And as for Tom Temple," continued Bob, blushing and grinning, "he's just a wonder. His poems are better than ever, and he's getting more money for them, and he's writing more. And only the other day he sent me another check for thirty dollars which he says he still owes me from our partnership on the Mississippi river."

"And he's one of the best friends you ever met?" said Mrs. Corcoran, her eyes dancing with fun.

"That's no joke," returned Bob. "The trouble with you, Mrs. Corcoran, is that you haven't seen these friends of mine."

"Well, Bob," said Mrs. Corcoran, rising. "I'm sure God's blessing is on you. I'm a better woman for knowing you "

"Oh, shucks!" interrupted the boy.

"I am. God knows I am. And I've promised Our Lord that in memory of the sweet charity shown my boy Angelo and my family I will give all the time I can spare and all the money I can spare to helping the needy. What has been done to me and mine I am going to do to those who, often without knowing it, take the place of Christ—the orphan, the widow, the stricken. As to that check for seventy-five dollars sent to Angelo, it all goes to charity. I am giving fifty of it to Father Carney to buy shoes for the poor boys and poor girls; and the other twenty-five I am holding for the help of any sick children, Bob, that you meet in your work as the Sick Committee."

"Mrs. Corcoran," said Bob, breaking into his most radiant smile, "you're just like my friends I've been talking about. And you're most like Mrs. John Symmes."

Then Mrs. Corcoran, glowing with pleasure, said, "Bob Ryan, if ever you want a home, come to me. My children, every one of them, love you as though you were my own true son."

"Why," exclaimed Bob, "that's just the way Mrs. John Symmes spoke to me. You certainly are her sister. Here—take her picture with you."

The tears came to Mrs. Corcoran's eyes. She accepted the photograph, and without saying a word (indeed, she was too full of emotion for utterance) she caught Bob's hand, and, leaning forward, imprinted a kiss upon his brow.

"And that," said Bob, deeply touched, "is what Mrs. Symmes did to me when she wished

me good-by. Mrs. Symmes is one of the best -Oh, gosh!"

With which prosaic expression ended the most sentimental passage thus far recorded in the story of Bob Ryan.

CHAPTER XI

Bob at the circus. A mysterious visitor. The Lady in Black once more.

THE most prosperous year in the history of St. Xavier School was drawing to a close. The spirit there prevailing was due largely to the spirit of the St. Aloysius Sodality and of the Children of Mary; and the spirit of these two Sodalities was in no small part due to the influence and initiative of Bob Ryan.

"I declare," said Father Carney, seated at his office desk, "never in my life—and it's gone considerably over a half a century—have I met such a wonderful small boy as Bob. He has the strength of ten, because his heart is pure; and he has the heart of ten, because there's something so big about him. The boy has a giant's strength, but he does not use it like a giant. He is gentle, yet absolutely fearless."

Brother Cyril, to whom he was talking, laughed.

"Did you hear of his adventure at the circus yesterday afternoon, Father?"

"No; what happened?"

"Well, I had all the acolytes there, thanks to your kindness in presenting the tickets "

"Don't put it on me, Brother," interrupted Father Carney. "It was the thoughtful Colonel Robert Bridwell who sent them to me. He's always thinking of somebody else's happiness. But please go on."

"Bob enjoyed the clowns so much that his laugh could be heard above the crowd. He was shiriingly happy. After a while, Father, all those clowns were acting as though Bob were the whole audience. Really, Father, I think that boy is a born leader of men. There were thousands of people there, but the circus actors, after the first two or three numbers, seemed to settle on Bob. Even the little girl equestrienne, a tiny mite of a thing with a very pretty and innocent face, made it a point to throw her smiles upon Bob."

"The boy," observed Father Carney, "has magnetism."

"There were some trained bears, comic fellows, natural-born clowns in every movement. Bob went simply wild over them. He seemed to fall in love with those bears."

"He's a wonder with cats and dogs," put in Father Carney. "Probably he's fond of all animals."

"After a while," the brother continued, "the bear trainer handed a large black bear a cigar, and said: 'Bruno, give this to the most popular man in the audience.' Just before he issued the orders, a man, evidently one of the company, had seated himself right in front of Bob. He was waiting to get that cigar. Did he get it? He did not. When the bear approached the man Bob gave a chuckle and made a slight clicking noise. And—would you believe it?— Bruno reached over the man's head and gave the cigar to Bob. But that wasn't all.

"Toward the end of the show one of the ringmasters brought out a bucking broncho, and offered five dollars to any boy who would ride it once around the ring. At first about one hundred boys seemed anxious to ride it; but after six brave youths had got on the beast, and got off much faster than they got on, the enthusiasm died out. Among others that changed their mind was Johnny O'Brien. He turned to Bob and urged him to try it. But Bob only grinned and shook his head. Now, when Johnny O'Brien wants something he wants it intensely. He returned to the charge. I was sitting behind the two, and so I could hear easily what he said. 'Bob,' urged Johnny, 'there's a family on Twelfth Street that's in bad. The father's sick, and his oldest girl is

worse, and they're short on the rent. Five dollars will put them up in business again/

"Then Bob stepped into the ring. 'Jump on, Johnny, quick,' said the ringmaster. But Bob walked up to the broncho, stroked its head, and seemed to whisper something in its ear. At once some sort of change came over the animal. Then Bob jumped on. And did the broncho hunch up and send Bob into the air? Well, yes, it did; but in a very mild way. Then Bob began talking to the beast, and the next thing you know that broncho trotted around the ring like a family pony."

"I've heard before of Bob's power over animals. They say he's a little St. Francis of Assisi; and I believe it. Do you know, Brother Cyril, that I envy that boy's kindness and power of love? I wish I knew how to deal with people as he does. He never gets fidgety or nervous or irritable as I do. Why, I'm a priest, and a priest's power for good is simply vast. But if I had his big heart I'd be able to do more good with less means than any man in Cincinnati."

"The fame of his work, Father, as a member of the Sick Committee has gone outside our parish. There are many families that when a child is sick send first for Bob, secondly for the priest, and if that doesn't stop the sickness they call in the doctor."

"I'm afraid," pursued Father Carney, "that he'll not be with us long."

"You mean he's going to St. Xavier's next year?"

"No; I think we're going to lose Bob. There's some sort of a mystery in his life, and I feel it in my bones that the mystery is soon to be cleared. I know the boy's story and I've kept track of him all this year, and I'm almost certain that something strange is going to occur."

"By the way, Lucille has written to Bob several times lately to be prepared for a big surprise. Do you think that has any bearing on Bob's case?"

"Yes; and Tom Temple has written to the same effect," answered the priest. "And I know that Tom takes a tremendous interest in Bob's case. All the same, Bob himself doesn't seem to worry."

"He's too busy to worry," said Brother Cyril. "What with his Sodality work and his studies and keeping up with his friends he's on the go all the time."

"And how is he getting on in class, Brother?"

"He's easily first. There's only one boy

who can touch him, and that's Albert Corcoran. Albert, in fact, is better than Bob in arithmetic. But in English, Bob is the best boy I've ever had in the eighth grade. He'll make a writer some day. Indeed, I should not be at all surprised if he should become a poet."

"A man," observed Father Carney, "who gets poetry into his life may not have time to get it into his writings. He certainly has the poetic heart '

"Which," quoted the Brother, "is more than all poetic art. Yes, Father, if I were a betting man, I'd be willing to stake everything I own or expect to own on Bob's coming out first in the contest for the scholarship at St. Xavier College."

"How are your boys getting along in their preparation?"

"They're going too hard, Father. Never in all my years of teaching did I have an easier time. Those boys, when I give them work, just eat it up. And Bob is the most eager of all. His eagerness is catching. Every day after our extra hour of class I have to drive them out. It's my happiest year of teaching."

"Brother," said Father Carney, "sometimes when I step within your class I almost envy you. It's simply wonderful to me to see how eager and alert and jolly and care-free your

boys are. They are so busy that one almost feels they are living ideal lives. They have so many good habits that they've no time to take up bad ones."

"Thank you, Father; you have paid me a great compliment. Well, in a few weeks the contest will come off. I hear that there will be about two hundred boys to take part, the pick of the eighth-grade boys in all our Cincinnati, Covington, and Newport parishes. No matter ; you just keep your eye on our boys. Good-by, Father."

On-that very afternoon, Bob, on arriving at his room after a very strenuous class-day, found his landlady awaiting him. She had the air of one with an important communication.

"Nobody sick, ma'am?" inquired Bob.

"No, Bob; but there's been a visitor to see you."

"Not Mrs. Corcoran?"

"I don't call Mrs. Corcoran a visitor. Why, isn't she here three times a week, going through everything in your room, and reading all your letters?"

Here it must be set down that Mrs. Jones, Bob's landlady, was a most excellent woman. She took the greatest interest in Bob, and she gave what time she could afford from her mul-

152 HIS LUCKIEST YEAR

tifarious duties to seeing to his comfort and happiness. But Mrs. Jones was a much overburdened woman; and many a time she had left many a thing undone for the boy because her more intimate duties absorbed her. So when Mrs. Corcoran, whose quick eye no household duty undone could escape, had come to her and begged as a favor for permission to visit Bob's room three or four times a week and go over the boy's clothes and linen and furniture, Mrs. Jones, because she was a noble woman, gave a willing consent; but because she was also just a woman she never quite forgave Mrs. Corcoran. Nor could she speak of that grateful friend of Bob's without saying something unkind. It was hard for Bob to understand.

"I'm sure she doesn't read my letters, Mrs. Jones," returned Bob gently. "She's not that kind. For that matter, if she wanted to read them, she'd be welcome. In fact, next time I see her I'm going to tell her she can read anything in my room."

"And have the whole parish talking about your private affairs?" protested Mrs. Jones indignantly. "Don't you do any such thing, Bob Ryan. She's got enough to talk about now from what she sees in your room, without her going and reading your private letters.

She's got a tongue, Mrs. Corcoran has. All women have."

It was difficult for Bob to follow this bit of what is called feminine logic. Here was a good woman declaring in one breath that Mrs. Corcoran read all his letters and in the other begging him not to give her permission, as she would be sure to make the contents known to every one. Bob did not as yet know that jealousy plays the mischief with logic.

"She's a splendid woman and you know it, ma'am," continued Bob.

"Oh, I'm not saying anything against her," answered the woman of the house. "But there's a lot of other people who would do what she does for you, and do it just as well, and see to your buttons and put your things in order; and then they wouldn't go boasting about it all over the street."

"But, Mrs. Jones, I'm sure she doesn't do that."

"Oh, you're young and innocent. But I have eyes and ears, and Alice O'Shea knows that she comes here, and so does Johnny O'Brien, and Elizabeth Reno. I've heard them talk about it."

"Good gracious!" exclaimed the boy, still smiling. "Of course they know it. So do their mothers and their sisters and their cousins

154 HIS LUCKIEST YEAR

and their aunts. Everybody on the street knows it."

"Just what I said," cried Mrs. Jones triumphantly.

"Yes; but I told them so myself, ma'am. Why, there's no secret about it."

Mrs. Jones laughed somewhat bitterly.

"Secret!" she echoed, "I should say not. That woman keep a secret! Oh, you don't understand people, Bob."

"Maybe I don't; but just the same, Mrs. Corcoran told me not to talk about her caring for my room. She wanted me to keep it quiet; but I felt so obliged to her that I just had to let it out. She's not to blame."

Mrs. Jones tossed her head and sniffed.

"Much you know about human nature," she stated with a tone of finality. "Some women talk about everything."

"I guess I know very little," commented the puzzled youth. "But who was the visitor?"

"Bob, it was some lady."

"Some lady?"

"Yes, some lady that I never laid eyes upon before. And there's no one upon the street that knows her."

"Why, did all the people on the street see her?"

"Oh, no; but after she left I went around and described her, and they all said she was a perfect stranger."

"Oh!" cried Bob, realizing with a suppressed grin that everybody on Pioneer Street was discussing his visitor. "Tell me all about her, please."

"She had beautiful grey eyes, Bob. Her hair was natural."

"Natural!" cried the boy.

"Yes, natural. Dull brown with little glints of gold in it. Her complexion was natu-ral-

"Natural!" cried Bob once more.

"Yes, natural. She had beautiful teeth. They were "

"Natural?" put in Bob.

"Yes," came the unsmiling but enthusiastic answer, "her teeth were natural, too. She had a beautiful mouth, small but curved like a Cupid's bow. There was a delicate color, like that of a peach, upon her cheeks. That color, Bob, was natural."

"Oh!" exclaimed Bob. "Of course it was natural; what would you expect it to be?"

Mrs. Jones cast a pitying smile upon Bob, and went on to tell how the lady's hair was dressed. Bob listened without comprehending. Then Mrs. Jones described the shoes the visitor wore, out of which description Bob

gleaned the information that there were shoes on both feet, and extremely small, size one and one-half. Every woman is a dressmaker at heart. Mrs. Jones, then, having disposed of the shoes, dilated upon the strange lady's dress. She spoke for five minutes. Women on the street had already heard the same description and had listened with delight. Bob, noble youth, lent an ear, too, and concealed his sufferings. He was listening to an unknown tongue. The hat and veil came in for their share of description.

"And," continued Mrs. Jones, "when I told her you weren't in she seemed to be so disappointed."

"Did you tell her to come back?"

"No; she said she couldn't; but," here Mrs. Jones reached a hand into the bosom of her shirt-waist and promptly brought out an envelope, a small square envelope, dainty, though somewhat rumpled, "she asked me to give you this."

Bob tore the flap open, pulled out the enclosure and read:

To Robert Ryan: The enclosed ten dollars is for flowers for sick little boys. Pray for the donor. M. L.

Then Bob, catching his breath, gazed now

upon the delicate handwriting, now upon the crisp ten-dollar note.

"It's ten dollars for flowers for the sick," he cried jubilantly. "Isn't that fine? But she doesn't sign her name."

"No," assented Mrs. Jones with unconcealed disappointment.

"I wonder who she was?" mused the boy.

"I've described her as well as I could, Bob."

Suddenly the boy's eyes gleamed.

"Say, Mrs. Jones, was she dressed in black?"

"Why, Bob Ryan, I spent ten minutes in telling you that."

"Oh, you did! And did she look sort of sad?"

"That's so; she did. Just like she'd lost her husband."

"And does she live outside the city?"

"She lives in Hamilton," came the answer. "She had to catch a train."

"Why didn't you tell me that?" cried Bob. "Oh, I'm so sorry I missed her. Why, Mrs. Jones, that's the Lady in Black."

"The Lady in Black!" echoed Mrs. Jones. "And who may be the Lady

Mrs. Jones found it useless to ask her question; for Bob had run up the stairs and bolted into his room, where, with his chin buried in his right hand, he meditated upon the mystery

of the lady whose love for the sick and friendless had once more come into his life.

Mrs. Jones meantime had stepped into the street, and before Bob's meditations were ended the ten-dollar note, the mysterious woman, and her missive with the initials were topics of discussion in ten different homes.

CHAPTER XII

So near and yet so far! The first meeting.

QUDDENLY Bob jumped to his feet. There O had flashed through his mind the thought that it was Thursday, his regular confession day, and that if he hurried over to the church he could catch his confessor before six o'clock, the dinner hour for both.

It was a beautiful afternoon. The street was bright with the latest rays of a glorious sun; there was a faint odor of flowers in the air; a bird, lost in a great city, sang his song from a telephone wire; and, best of all, the street was a thing of joy with the sweet cries and happy laughter and swift movement and artless prattle of boys and girls—as nice a set of children, Bob fondly meditated, as one could find from Oakland to New York.

Prominent among them were Alice O'Shea and her dearest friend in the world, Elizabeth Reno. The two were walking up and down the street, not without some show of stateli-ness, marred somewhat, it must be confessed, by the fact that each had a fast-disappearing ice-cream cone. They were the belles of the

street, the belles, that is, of the extremely

younger set; and they were dressed accordingly. Alice's curls —"almost natural"— set off her features to the best advantage. Dressed in white, dashed with touches of blue, she looked like a princess such as one would see looking out from magic casements in joy land. Dark-haired Elizabeth, with her clear-cut features, her large and expectant eyes, and her slow smile, dressed, allowing for a dash of red, to a dot like her dearest friend, was a splendid foil to her companion.

"Where are you going, Bob?" inquired Alice.

"I'm going to get shriven."

"Is it good to eat?" continued the young lady.

"I mean," laughed the boy, "that I'm going to confession."

"We went this afternoon, early," said Elizabeth. "And," she added proudly, "we both got up early last Saturday and went to communion."

"And," put in Alice, "we're going again next Saturday."

"Yes"— here Elizabeth took up the wondrous strain—"and we intend to keep it up just as long as the fine weather lasts."

"That's fine!" said Bob.

"And do you know, Bob," continued Alice,

"that we're all friends on this street? I speak to all the girls now, and so does Elizabeth."

"It's been going on that way for eight weeks," explained Elizabeth, her eyes as she spoke betraying the wonder of it all; "and my sister Catharine has got us all so interested in the Ladies of the Blessed Sacrament Section. They say she'll be the next prefect."

"Say, Bob," Alice inquired with tense interest, "do you think there's a chance for me to be prefect some day?"

Bob was about to answer, when the young ladies, screaming with excitement and forgetting that they were dressed for the evening, darted down the street. Johnny O'Brien had just opened a box of candy for the benefit of his many friends.

Bob went on, feeling intensely happy. Spring and peace and love and kindness— were they not all about him? The chimes of St. Xavier Church were announcing to Cincinnati that the time was half after five when Bob reached the corner of Sixth and Sycamore. A car had stopped to take on passengers. As the car started, the boy, turning from Sycamore to Sixth, glanced casually in its direction. From the arms of a woman who had just got on slipped a small package. In the very moment that Bob saw the mishap he

took action. He ran into the street, picked up up the package, and, still running, caught up with the car.

"Here you are, ma'am," he cried, handing it to the lady.

"Oh, thank you so much I"

Bob was thrilled with the sweetness of the voice; and, for the first time, he looked into its owner's face. The face and the voice belonged together. There was sweetness in both — and sadness. As the car moved on the woman turned and looked at Bob. Suddenly her eyes lighted up, she drew a deep breath, and a smile came upon her fair and delicate features which dispelled as though by magic every trace of sorrow. No less electrical was the effect on Bob. He smiled in return and waved a hand, while there surged through him a feeling of vague longing. It all happened in a few seconds. The face, the lovely face, the face with an indescribable something which stirred the boy's whole being profoundly, was gone.

Bob entered the church wondering. He made his confession, and in due time went once more into the pure air of sunset, still wondering.

Suddenly he paused on the church steps and gave a gasp.

"By George!" he exclaimed. "Why didn't I jump on that car and introduce myself? Why didn't I notice her dress? I must have noticed it or I wouldn't know it now. It was the Lady in Black."

CHAPTER XIII

In which chanty interferes with study, Bob is awaiting surprising news, and the great examination day is at hand.

IT was the eve of the great examination. Bob Ryan and Albert Corcoran were met to do their last bit of preparation. Albert was the picture of good health. Bob looked tired, as his friend noticed.

"What's the matter, Bob? You don't look like yourself."

"I don't feel like myself, Albert. There's a little boy on Pendleton Street, one of the nicest little boys you ever met. He's in the fifth grade and the brightest in the class."

"You mean Charlie Fitzpatrick, the new altar-boy?"

"That's the boy. You see, I helped Charlie learn his Mass prayers, and we got to know each other pretty well. He's so frail and delicate it used to make me feel ashamed of myself. I've only known him a few weeks—not more than three—and he's one of the best friends "

A giggle stopped Bob's flow of language.

"Well, he is," pursued Bob stoutly. "Yesterday, early in the evening, his little sister,

Mary, who in her way is just as fine as he is, came running here to tell me that he was awful sick, and wanted me to come and see him. Of course I went."

"Don't I know it?" put in Albert. "When I came here to go over the cube root with you I found your room empty. I stayed for two hours."

"Awfully sorry," said Bob.

"You needn't be; I studied just the same, and went home ready for any examination. But what about little Charlie?"

"Say, Albert, it was awful. I never saw anybody in such pain. I stayed with him till away after ten; and it broke me all up to see how terribly that little fellow could suffer and keep on smiling. When I left him he was feeling ever so much better. But I tell you, Albert, I wasn't. I felt as if I had been sick; and I couldn't sleep for over three hours, thinking of that poor little chap."

"No wonder you look all in."

"I wish I were sick in his place," said Bob. "I'm strong. I could stand it. But he is so frail, and yet so brave. Father Carney brought him communion this morning. The poor kid, his sister told me, was burning up with thirst all night; but he wouldn't touch a drop of water after it struck twelve."

"Oh, that reminds me," said Albert. "Father Carney said a funny thing the other day. He said that when he first took charge of the school years ago, children, when they took very sick, always asked for a priest to hear their confession; but now that frequent communion has come in they never say a word about confession, but ask for a priest to bring them Holy Communion."

"Little children are so interesting 1" observed Bob Ryan, age fourteen. "But," he added, "some grown people are very interesting, too. "I've got the funniest letters from Tom and Lucille. Tom is in New York and Lucille is in Iowa. Both of them tell me that next time I hear from them, and it won't be very long, I will hear the most wonderful news. And both of them want me to pray hard for their intention till July the fifth. I wonder what's up?"

"July the fifth!" exclaimed Angelo, jumping to his feet. "Why, don't you see?"

"See what? They want me to offer up my communion for a special intention on that day."

"Bob, what an owl you are. Don't you remember what you told me? July the nfth is the day your father threw you out!'

"By George!" said Bob. "I never thought of that."

"And—' continued Angelo, "he told you not to dare come back to Dubuque for one year. On July the fifth your year is up. Bob, I'll bet anything that Tom Temple, who has been studying your case, has found out something, or expects to find out something on that date."

"I wonder," said Bob. "Anyhow, my year will be up, and if I can afford it I'm going back to Dubuque to see all my friends."

"And when you get to Dubuque, Bob, how long do you intend staying?"

"That depends," Bob made answer. "If I win a scholarship I'm coming back here, even if I have to tramp it. I suppose I can get some work to do after school hours. I'll have to. I'm going to be poor next year."

"You'll stay with us," cried Albert. "My mother wants it; my brother Angelo wants it; and, as for my sisters, they all want it; and little Rosie is crying for it."

"It's mighty nice of your mother, Albert," returned Bob, "but I can't do it. Everybody's been helping me, and I'm afraid, if it keeps on, I'll be pauperized. It seems to me I'm big enough and strong enough to make

my own way. It spoils a chap to be relying on his friends for everything. Anyhow, I may not win the scholarship; and if I don't-

"Well, what if you don't?"

"Why, I think I'll stay in Dubuque and try to earn my living there. That's my home, and I feel that I ought to be there."

"Did my mother show you the letter she got from Mrs. John Symmes, Bob?"

"Yes; and I got one, too. Mrs. Symmes says she's the happiest woman in the world. She's so proud of you and Angelo and your sisters. And she thinks that it's most extraordinary that I should find in Cincinnati her sister, and that I should be such a close friend of your family. And best of all, she's going to return to the Church she was baptized in. It's funny, Albert, that I didn't notice from the start how much alike your mother and Mrs. Symmes were. When I saw your mother first I had a feeling that there was something familiar about her; but I couldn't make out where it came in."

"In that letter my mother got," said Albert, "she begs her to come and pay her a visit. Mrs.

Symmes wants my mother to bring on all the children and stay the summer. And it won't cost my mother a cent, either."

"That will be fine. I hope your mother will go"

"So do I, Bob; my mother hasn't had a vacation in twenty years; and she's pretty tired. This past year has been very hard on her. I was sick for two months, and Angelo for ten weeks, and my father died. It was just one thing after another. We all want her to go, even if the rest of us stay home. But she can't make up her mind. Last night she said that if I win the scholarship she'll go, and she'll take me along for a good rest."

Bob cupped his chin, supporting his right elbow with his left hand.

"Say," he said presently. "Suppose I win, you lose that trip."

"That's what I said to my mother. And she said that since St. Xavier School could win only one scholarship she'd go provided my average was among the first five."

"Good," cried Bob. "And I think you'll come first, anyhow."

"You're the only one who does think that way, Bob. Brother Cyril thinks you'll make the best examination of any boy he has ever taught, and all the fellows feel sure that you'll come out first."

"I think, Albert, that I'm pretty well ready for anything except that confounded old cube

brute. It is a brute, and no mistake. Suppose we go over that. You know it; and then we'll run over the last ten pages of our English grammar."

Albert did his best to initiate Bob into the inner workings of extracting the cube root. Bob, though he tried to listen, had no little difficulty in keeping his eyes open.

"There 1" said Albert after twenty minutes of figuring and explanation. "Do you see it now?"

There was no answer. Albert turned his eyes upon Bob's face. Bob, sitting upright in his chair and with an air of attention, was fast asleep.

"Hey, Bob!"

"Oh!" cried Bob, jumping up and shaking his head. "I beg your pardon, Albert. I didn't know I was asleep. How far did we get with that sum?"

Albert, with a laugh, began his explanations once more, and Bob, pinching himself from time to time to keep awake, paid close attention.

"Now, Bob," asked Albert presently, "do you get it?"

"I think so," returned Bob. "There's one little point, though, I'm not quite so sure of."

At that moment there was a timid knock at the door.

"Come in," shouted Bob. "Why," he went on as a rather frightened little girl stood revealed at the threshold, "is that you, Mary Fitzpatrick?"

"Please, Bob, my brother's been took bad again; and he wants you. He's awfully sick, and he wants you."

Bob forgot all about the examination.

"Say, Albert, suppose you come along, too. I've just got to go."

"All right, Bob; and when we come back we can settle that little matter of the cube root."

The three accordingly hurried out into the night.

Their visit did great good. Bob succeeded in consoling and strengthening the little sufferer. The paroxysm of pain passed; and at eleven o'clock the two boys set back for Pioneer Street.

But there was no more studying that night. Bob, thoroughly exhausted, excused himself and went promptly to bed.

CHAPTER XIV

Bob's failure, the comments of Mr. Latvian thereon, and the unhappy results.

ON the following day, a few minutes before noon, there was, for the first time since the day after the Christmas holidays, deep gloom in the eighth-grade classroom. The twenty-four boys who had represented the class in the interparochial contest were just returned, looking like anything but victors. Bob Ryan had lost his usual smile.

"Well, boys," said Brother Cyril, "how were the questions?"

"Rotten," answered Edward Bolan.

"Some of them were pretty hard," added Albert Corcoran. "There was a very hard sentence to parse and analyze, and I just hope I got it. The arithmetic was dead easy."

A protesting growl arose from twenty-three throats.

"I guess," said Bob, whose eyes were heavy, "that it was easy for Albert. Anything in arithmetic is easy to him. But one of the problems nearly broke my head."

"One of 'em," cried Bolan, "just broke my heart. I left the old thing out."

"Did you manage to get it, Bob?" asked the brother.

"I don't know. Brother. I believe I got most of it: but I'm not sure about one part."

"And how about the composition?"

"Oh/ said Bob, "we were told to write a page and a half or two about 'An Early Spring Morning in the Country."

"That's just your line, Bob."

"Yes; but somehow I felt heavy and tired, and I never knew before how hard it was to think. I wrote a page and a half; but I think it was punk."

Deeper grew the gloom upon the entire class.

"Let's do something to cheer ourselves up," observed a wag. "There was a funeral at St. Xavier's at ten o'clock. Brother, if we took a car right now we might get to the cemetery in time for the burial. I'm sure a little thing like that would lighten the gloom."

Bob was the only one present to laugh heartily.

"Oh, well," said Brother Cyril, "you needn't be discouraged, boys. After all, it's better to deserve to succeed than to succeed."

The class received this information with unbroken mournfulness.

"You've done your duty," continued Brother Cyril ; "and that's the thing that counts."

"Say, Brother," said the wag, no suspicion of a smile upon his countenance, "I don't see that just now. I'm awfully stupid to-day. So are all of us. Would you mind making a diagram on the board, so we could all understand it "

The Brother laughed. The effect was as though a burst of sunshine had broken the gloom of a cloudy day.

"Boys, boys," pleaded Brother Cyril, "don't take on so. By the way, how did the boys from the other schools feel after the examination?"

"They looked just as sad as we did," answered Bob.

"Ah!" cried the brother, much consoled. "Did they seem to be very gloomy?"

"Gloomy isn't the word for it, Brother Cyril," Albert made answer.

"They looked," said the wag, "as they'd just spent a week in the trenches and were going back again."

"Some of them that I saw," added Bolan, "looked as though they had just been through an earthquake and come out just alive enough to know they weren't killed."

A great joy was growing on Brother Cyril's face.

"Did they seem to feel absolutely

wretched?" he asked with the light of rosy hope in his eyes.

"They did," roared the twenty-four.

Whereupon everybody present broke into smiles. The gloom was dispelled; a holiday spirit prevailed, and Brother Cyril, having first consulted with the head Brother, announced that they would have a picnic at Burnet Woods the next day.

When, a few minutes later, the twenty-four contestants filed into the school-yard, each carried himself as though he were a wedding guest.

A week passed by before the result of the contest was announced. On the morning of July first all the contestants, two hundred and eighteen in number, assembled in the Memorial Hall of St. Xavier College.

On the stage stood Father Feeley, the vice-president of the college, and Father Dalton, one of the professors.

"Boys," began Father Feeley, "I've no doubt that most of you thought the examination was very severe. It was. We made it a searching examination, because we had reason to believe that you were the brightest set of contestants that had ever entered into our scholarship contest. Had we made the examination an easier one, we feared that it

176 HIS LUCKIEST YEAR

would be difficult to find out the winners. There would be, we thought, too many ties. Now, the event would seem to justify our judgment. Hard as the examination has been, there are two almost tied for the first place, and three for the fifth place."

At this announcement many of the boys began to bob up and down in their seats like corks upon troubled waters.

"I see," continued Father Feeley, "that you are all bursting to get results. Before I proceed to announce the winners, I think it right to tell you that neither I nor any one connected with the college has, as yet, the least idea as to who are going to enjoy the privilege of the first scholarship. Each of you, as you know, signed your examination papers with a fictitious name. Each of you placed in an envelope signed with your assumed name a slip of paper containing your real name. These envelopes are still sealed. And now I shall proceed to announce the winners according to the names they adopted for the occasion.

"The highest average, entitling the boy who gained it to a scholarship both for high school and college, was won by 'Blue Hope.' While Father Dalton is verifying the winner, suppose the boy who adopted that name

There was a tremendous sensation when a handsome, dark-eyed boy arose.

"Albert Corcoran!" shouted Bob.

"Corcoran! Corcoran!" yelled the eighth-grade pupils of St. Xavier School. "Xavier! Xavier!"

"His average," continued Father Feeley when the applause had died out, "is ninety-nine and one-third per cent."

This announcement evoked buzzes of admiration.

"The next in merit," continued the vice-president, "has an average of ninety-nine and a quarter per cent. Between the two, you will observe, is just the difference of one-twelfth of a note. He uses the name 'Campion.'"

Then Bob arose.

There was applause; but it was not hearty. Bob's classmates had felt so sure of his leading the class that they were unable at once to put aside their disappointment. His very popularity was the cause of the scant enthusiasm. Bob did not know how much he was loved; but he realized with a sensitiveness new to him that there was a marked difference between the ovation accorded Albert and the faint plaudits which had greeted him.

"Why," exclaimed Father Feeley, "this is a great surprise. The two leaders are both

from St. Xavier School. As I presume you all know, only one scholarship is awarded to any school. The next winner, with a percentage of ninety-six, is 'Comus.' '

A boy from the Assumption Parish arose.

"The next in merit is 'Tom Sawyer,' average ninety-five and a half."

Walter Godfrey, the wag of Brother Cyril's class, arose. He, too, received an ovation.

"The next in merit is 'Macbeth,' average ninety-five."

Edward Bolan received a round of applause little less hearty than Godfrey's.

The third scholarship finally fell to a pupil of the Cathedral Parish of Covington, the fourth to St. Edward's, and the fifth to St. Francis de Sales'.

Bob left the hall with a feeling of depression for which he could not account. No one rejoiced more than he at the signal victory of Albert Corcoran ; and yet there was associated with it a sinking of the heart. Surely, he reasoned, he could not be jealous. His classmates were showering congratulations upon Albert, and they did it in a whole-souled way. But they seemed to fight shy of Bob; they addressed him awkwardly; they were quick to slip away from his presence.

"Bob Ryan," said Brother Cyril, catching

his hand at the door of the hall, "if you had only got one little point right in that cube-root problem you'd have won with a rating of ninety-nine and four-fifths per cent."

"Is that so, Brother?" asked the boy, trying, with faint success, to smile.

"Yes; Father Feeley has just told me. It's too bad. Albert Corcoran got the arithmetic perfectly. He lost two-thirds of a note in English composition. What a pity you missed a simple thing like that!"

For the first time in many a month Bob was, as the saying is, under the weather. Hard study in preparation for the contest, some Worry about his finances, which were almost exhausted, and his vigil of several nights in succession at the bedside of his little sick friend had all united to put him into a state of nerves. It came to him, as Brother Cyril addressed him, that he would not have missed a single fraction of a note had he not gone to visit little Fitzpatrick the night before the examination. Moreover, he was quite sure that the Brother, no less than his classmates, was disappointed. In fact, he read in the Brother's words an expression of chagrin which was not there at all. Bob hurried home, locked his door and went to bed, where he remained till supper.

While Bob, really ill, though he knew it not, passed the better part of the day in broken slumber, several things happened which concerned him intimately.

Word of the wonderful success of St. Xavier School spread rapidly. It reached, first of all, the office of the Catholic Telegraph. The editor, a St. Xavier boy himself, rose to" the occasion. It struck him that a contest of such a nature, in which two boys of the same school came within a tiny fraction of each other and both within a small fraction of absolute perfection, was worth special notice. He resolved to secure, if possible, the photographs of the two and to reproduce them in the next number of his paper.

The news a few minutes later reached the people of St. Xavier Parish. One of the first to get it was a pleasant-faced, grey-haired man on the confines of the period which separates middle life from old age. He was a bank-teller by occupation. In his early years William Lawton had been the handsomest and most engaging man in St. Xavier Parish. His manners were unusually winning. A student of St. Xavier College, he had shown in his sophomore year a strong desire to enter the priesthood. He was not the brightest boy of his class, but he possessed sufficient talent to

give promise of qualifying in those studies required of a seminarian. In addition, his affability, his natural kindliness and his conversational powers led those interested in him to believe that he would make a priest with extraordinary power for good. At the last moment, yielding to the tears and pleading of his mother, he abandoned his intention of going to the seminary, and, leaving college, went to work in a clerical position. His life, from that hour, was made up of little things. Slowly but surely his high ideals melted away, and he became a commonplace man with fine manners and a misplaced sense of humor. The one thing he picked out in the doings and sayings of his friends and acquaintances was the ridiculous side. As the years went on he became a gossip; and at the time he enters into this story he was never known to say a kind word of any one, unless by way of introduction to some bit of scandal. William Lawton is a sad case of progressive deterioration; and it is depressing to reflect that we meet our William Lawton in every community.

He lived in the home of a widow, Mrs. Alma Gentry, whose only son was a pupil in the eighth grade of St. Xavier School.

When Lawton came in for noon lunch Mrs.

Gentry at once acquainted him with the news of Bob's failure.

"Too bad, isn't it?" said Lawton, addressing himself to his soup. "That boy's had it all his own way ever since he came here. Think of an absolute stranger, a lad of fourteen, camping in our parish and taking possession of it! The boys elect him prefect of their Sodality, and they know nothing about him."

"He's the strongest boy in the school," observed Malcolm Gentry.

"So he is," answered Lawton with a genial chuckle. "In fact, I shouldn't be at all surprised if his father were a prizefighter or a professional gymnast. But of course we don't know anything about his parents. The people of St. Xavier's are very charitable. The boy is pretty fat. It may come out some day that his father was a strong man who married the Fat Lady in the same circus."

All this, with perfect charm of manner and with his most winning smile, did Mr. Lawton blandly declare. He attended Mass every Sunday and considered himself a good Catholic. Let us trust that he sometimes begged to be delivered from his hidden sins.

"At any rate," Mrs. Gentry announced, "I'm glad that one of our own parish and not a boy of unknown origin and a stranger is the winner."

The widow made this statement from the fullness of her heart. She had never forgiven Bob for having been elected prefect of the Sodality. By some course of intricate reason she persuaded herself that, had it not been for Bob's invasion into St. Xavier Parish, her boy might have been the recipient of that high office. Malcolm's record hardly justified her hopes. It seemed to be the rule of his life to let neither study nor duty of any kind interfere with his amusements. Thus, early in life he had developed a strong taste for cheap cigarettes and cheap theaters. His mother held that Brother Cyril did not understand her darling.

"Yes, it's better so," assented Lawton. "At the same time, Mrs. Gentry, we must be fair to Bob Ryan. Of course, he's overrated. Boys always make too much of pure animal strength, and most people are taken by that vacant grin of his. He's got a loud laugh, too. People like it; but people don't know that Oliver Goldsmith speaks of the 'loud laugh that speaks the vacant mind.' When all is said, however, it must be granted that the boy has many fine qualities. Without friend or guardian, living alone, he has certainly done

very well. He's behaved right decently. He had every chance to run around and dissipate. And he had lots of money. It's a wonder he's not completely ruined. Where does that money of his come from?"

"I'm sure I don't know," replied Mrs. Gentry.

"It comes easy," observed Malcolm, "for it goes easy."

"I repeat, then/' continued Lawton in his softest and kindest tones, "that we must give him all credit for going through the year unspoiled, and even if during the past few weeks he has changed for the worse "

"What's that?" cried the widow, glowing with excitement.

"Of course," whispered Lawton, "this talk of ours is confidential."

"You may count on my prudence, Mr. Law-ton; I detest gossip."

Mr. Lawton grinned. He had another story to tell at the bank.

"A few nights ago," continued the teller, "I happened to be coming down Sycamore Street at about twelve o'clock, and whom should I run up against but Bob Ryan. He was walking along with his head down, as though he didn't want to be recognized."

"Isn't that too bad!" ejaculated the widow,
her tones rich in sadness, her eyes gleaming with joy and interest.

"I wouldn't for anything in the world wrong the boy," Mr. Lawton went on, "but it struck me that his gait was the least little bit uncertain."

"Mercy!" gasped the widow. "So young and given to drink!"

"Now, now, don't say that; it's a serious charge, Mrs. Gentry. I hate to believe such a thing. I saw him the next day, and his face didn't look quite right. That very night, I've learned— the night before the contest—he went out again, and he was up late. This morning I saw him, and his face looked worse than it did yesterday, and his eyes looked suspiciously like they were bloodshot."

"Poor boy!" exclaimed the enraptured woman. "Who knows but he is being led astray."

"Don't jump at conclusions, Mrs. Gentry. Remember, too, that people can go wrong without being led astray. Some children are born into this world with tainted blood. They go wrong, and only God Himself may judge how far they are responsible. But a thousand suspicions do not make a certainty." Here Mr. Lawton arose, adjusted his collar, and with his best smile, added:

"You should have seen that boy this morning. I got one look at his face, and it was the face of 'the morning after the night before/'

And the kindly-spoken, kindly-eyed teller departed.

Then up rose Mrs. Gentry with haste.

"Malcolm, dear, if you stay at home and do the dishes I'll be back in an hour and will give you fifty cents."

Fifty cents! Malcolm's face showed enthusiasm.

"Say, ma, make it sixty."

"All right, Malcolm."

Putting on her best hat and her special gloves, Mrs. Gentry hurried out to visit her friends.

Two hours after her departure there were twelve women, every one of them a gossip, who were armed with the following information:

Bob Ryan was the son of a prizefighter who had drunk himself to death and of a Fat Lady who gave promise of repeating her husband's performance. Bob Ryan had come to Cincinnati to reform. He had made a brave fight for nine months. But the forces of heredity were too strong, and so for the past four weeks he had been going the way of his parents. No wonder, then, that he had failed in winning the scholarship. Three weeks ago his teacher

had been certain of the boy's victory. It was really too bad. The boy was more to be pitied than censured; still, he was hardly a fit companion for the innocent little children of the parish.

It was a great day for the gossips. Some of them were having the time of their lives. Not all, however; the door was shown to several of them.

But—alas for human nature—Bob was suffering from his too great popularity. There were men and women who knew him only by reputation, and they entertained for him something of the sentiment which the Athenians conceived for Aristides. After all, who was he? Who were his parents?

Those who knew him were indignant. Did not Jerry, the janitor of St. Xavier School, pull Mr. Lawton's nose? Did not William Devine, forgetting his good resolutions, soundly thrash Malcolm Gentry, and send him home with a swollen nose and a discolored eye? Did not Mrs. Corcoran request the gossip of Ellen Street never more to darken the Corcoran doors?

Before nightfall Alice O'Shea, Elizabeth Reno, and Mary Fitzgerald were no longer on speaking terms with fifteen of their girl friends. In a word, a good part of the parish,

188 HIS LUCKIEST YEAR

thanks to Lawton and other old women, was set by the ears.

Bob slept during most of these strenuous hours. He awoke refreshed at five o'clock. Half an hour later Mrs. Corcoran arrived, bringing with her the entire family. She was determined that Bob should not go out on the street that night.

"We're going to celebrate, Bob,*' she said, with a smile so full of sympathy and tenderness that Bob felt almost instinctively that she felt sorry for him. "You and my boy Albert have set the record for St. Xavier School. I've told your landlady that I'll set up the supper for to-night. We've brought everything along, and we'll have our supper right in this room."

It was a quiet celebration. How kind, how tender, they all were to Bob 1 He could sense as never before their love. But there was something more. They pitied him. The tears came to Bob's eyes, tears manfully suppressed. After all, it was a wondrous thing to have the love of this wonderful family. Bob had never met a family like it. The Reades were wonderful, too; but they were rich. The Cor-corans, poor and struggling, had the special mark that made them most like to Our Lord. And yet, why should they pity him? And

then, he reflected, the boys of his class had been so cold! Could it be possible that he had disgraced himself by coming out second? The question seemed, on the face of it, absurd.

The Corcorans stayed till ten o'clock. Before leaving, Albert engaged to meet Bob the next morning at half-past eight. They were to go together to William Anthony's photographic studio on Fourth Street to have their pictures taken for the Catholic Telegraph.

Mrs. Corcoran bade Bob a most affectionate farewell. Her smile was beautiful as she gazed on him at the threshold; but as the door closed on her she burst into a fit of weeping which fairly appalled her children.

Never before had they seen her lose her self-control.

She was herself presently. The children walked on in awed silence.

Then Mrs. Corcoran said as though to herself:

"It is a beautiful world. It is! There may be hundreds of foul tongues, but a boy like Bob Ryan, brave, noble, loyal, unselfish, atones a hundred times over for them all."

CHAPTER XV

In which Bob has his picture taken, with, as the sequel will show, extraordinary results.

"T TEY, Bob —ready?"

11 Albert Corcoran, standing at the partly open door of Bob's room, was grinning genially.

Bob, frowning slightly, was seated at his desk and sorting his letters. They were, alas, old letters. Anita's weekly missive had not come. There was no word from the Reades, none from Tom Temple. The postman had just passed down the street. Bob was surprised and disappointed. Matt Morris should have written, too; but he could account for Matt's failure. Campion College had just dismissed its students, and Matt, very likely, was engrossed in preparations for camp life. For ten months Bob had been receiving letters on an average of four a week, and now seven days had passed without a word from his dear absent friends. In addition, on reckoning up his expense account and his cash on hand, the disturbing fact stood clear that when all outstanding bills were paid he would have not more than four or five dollars with which to face the world. There were other matters troubling him, too, to be presently revealed to Albert.

"Say, Albert," he observed as they came out upon Pioneer Street, "do the fellows think I'm to blame because I didn't get one hundred per cent?"

"Nonsense, Bob; what put that into your head? They're sorry, that's all. What makes you ask such a question?"

"Well, somehow they act like it. By George, I'm afraid I'm getting suspicious. And maybe I'm spoiled. You know, Albert, everybody's been so kind to me that I just take their smiles and goodness as a matter of course, instead of wondering at it. Now this morning after five o'clock Mass several of the acolytes who were to serve at six o'clock came in. Now, the funny thing is they were kind and nice, all right, but, without intending it, they hurt my feelings. Two or three stood apart and looked at me in a strange way, and talked in whispers. It's a terrible thing to become suspicious, but for the life of me I couldn't help thinking they were talking about me."

"Don't get suspicious, Bob," said Albert, knowing only too well that Bob's inferences were fully justified. "It isn't at all like you.

192 HIS LUCKIEST YEAR

As for friends, you've got more just now than you could shake a stick at."

"I should never forget that," said Bob simply. "Often it makes me feel utterly mean and contemptible when I think of all the boys and girls and people who show such trust in me. Why, only this morning Brother Crellin went out of his way to congratulate me. He told me that I had done wonderfully well, and he was proud of me. And there was so much kindness in his voice. There was something else, Albert."

"What else?"

"There was pity. And yesterday evening, when you and your mother and the others of your family were over, I noticed that, too. You were all sorry for me."

Albert was about to make an evasive answer, when a clear, sweet, piercing high voice crying, "Bob, Bob!" saved the situation.

Turning, the two discovered, running after them at full speed, Alice and Elizabeth.

"Hey, Bob! Are you going to have your picture took?" panted Alice.

"Now, who told you that?" cried Bob, breaking once more into the smile concerning which Lawton had quoted Oliver Goldsmith's much-abused line. Alice always awoke the boy's best smile. It was good to see her, fair, curly-

headed, radiant, the kindness of a kind soul shining out of kind blue eyes.

"Who told me?—Johnny O'Brien, of course."

"Johnny O'Brien," remarked Elizabeth, looking upon Bob with her most favoring eyes, "knows everything."

"How could he have known it?" asked Bob.

"The answer's easy," responded Albert, laughing heartily. "Johnny saw me in my Sunday best coming to get you a while ago, and it takes Johnny to put two and two together."

All this time the fair Alice was holding daintily in her fingers a beautiful red rose. At this point of the conversation Elizabeth nudged Alice, who, looking darkly, began making signals in return.

"Wait, Bob," she commanded, and she drew Elizabeth aside. They communed together earnestly, and in low tones. Finally, advancing to Bob's side, Alice, with a pretty blush, said: "Bob, take this rose and wear it in your buttonhole while you're getting your picture took."

"It's from both of us," announced Elizabeth, blushing in turn.

"Oh, thank you, thank you!" exclaimed the radiant Bob.

194 HIS LUCKIEST YEAR

Then the two young ladies fell to nudging each other and to making extraordinary signs.

"You tell him," said Alice.

"You tell him," returned Elizabeth.

"Let's both do it," suggested the blonde.

"That's it. We'll both do it. Now together."

Alice held up her hand. The two, still blushing, faced Bob.

"Follow me," whispered Alice, taking the lead, and obeyed so promptly by the quick Elizabeth that they seemed to utter each syllable synchronously— —

"Bob— Ryan—when—you— get— your picture — took — will — you— give— me— one?" upon delivering which they suddenly turned and ran screaming away.

"By Jove," said Bob, as they turned into Broadway, at the end of Pioneer Street, "those two girls are wonders. They're as good as real boys, only they're funnier. You're right, Albert, I guess I'm suspicious. And," he added, "I'm spoiled, too. Albert, those two girls talked to me, and gave me this beautiful rose—and they didn't notice you the whole time. And it didn't seem strange to me at all. I guess I'm getting selfish."

"Not at all," returned Albert stoutly. "They hardly know me, anyhow; and besides

I've got a flower in my buttonhole; and if I'd been as kind and thoughtful as those two little girls I'd have-Albert's flow of language was brought to a sudden halt by Eva Conlon, a little girl of the primary grade. She was a simple, innocent, loving little child, as are nearly all the little ones of that grade in St. Xavier's. To inhale the mystic fragrance of paradise one has only to watch these little ones going about the ordered duties of the classroom. The miracle of it all is to account for the loveliness which is the atmosphere in which these little ones live and move and have their being. Not all of them come by it honestly. Eva's mother was decidedly unlike her child.

The mother was on a shopping tour, and Eva, with unequal stride, was trotting on beside her. Happening to glance around, Eva perceived Bob. Uttering a scream of sheer delight, she turned and ran at full speed toward him. It looked as though she would run Bob down. But little children have the peculiar gift of making a flying start and coming to a stand with equal suddenness.

"Oh, Bob!" cried Eva, with shining eyes, as she caught his hand. And that was all Eva had to say—the rest was expression. "How do you do, Eva?" said the boy.

"Here, Eva," cried the mother, darting a malignant glance at Bob, as she shouldered the child away, "don't talk to everybody you meet on the street. It's common."

Then as she walked off with the wide-eyed child she added in a tone that came distinctly to Bob's ears—

"Before I let my child associate with strangers I'd like to know first something about their fathers and mothers—if they've got any."

Had the woman struck Bob in the face he could have borne it better. His head went down, his face grew red and then deadly pale. Tears sprang to his eyes. As for Albert, the volatile, easy, good-natured Albert, he too was much moved. His eyes blazed, his mouth quivered. Placing his hands on his knees, he stared at the woman's back, with a stare which, had it been a dagger, would have pierced her through, making at the same time a face that would have done credit to a Gorgon. Albert went through with all this in much less time than it takes to tell. Then he turned his sympathetic attention to his companion.

"Bob, Bob!" he cried, putting his arm through his companion's; "don't you pay any attention to that—that—cat!"

"Albert," returned Bob simply, "that was awful. I never thought of such a thing. No one ever said anything like that to me in all my born days."

"Forget it, Bob."

"Oh!" cried Bob, "I see it all now. They've been talking about me. That's why you all looked so sorry."

"Yes, Bob," admitted Albert, "an old woman of this parish who wears trousers started the talk. But don't you mind. You've lots of friends."

"How can I help minding," cried Bob, choking back a sob. "If they'd abuse me I think I could stand for it. But they've—they've been talking about my mother."

Albert could say nothing. But he caught Bob's hand and pressed it.

"I don't even remember her," said Bob; "but she's been always the same to me as my guardian angel. In fact, I think of them always at the same time. All this year, Albert, I've been helped to do right and fight temptation because I believe that my mother, who died when I was a baby, is a saint in heaven watching over me."

"That's what my mother believes, too," said Albert.

"Last night or early this morning," continued Bob, drawn out of his ordinary reticence by the hideous insult of the woman, "I

had the loveliest dream. It seemed to me that as I was half-asleep, half awake, a veiled figure walked into my room. She came close to my bed, and I saw her face—the loveliest face! I felt that it was the loveliest face, though I couldn't describe it. And that face bent down to mine, and I knew that it was my mother. I knew it just as I know you're Albert. And her lips touched mine. Then I woke and I was crying 'mother!' with my arms stretched out to embrace her. There was no sign of her in my room. But, Albert, I felt as though she had certainly been there."

"That's just beautiful," continued Albert. "You ought to tell Father Carney. Maybe your mother did come to you in a dream to make you brave in spite of all this horrid talk."

As Albert was finishing his sentence they were tramping up the stairs which led to Mr. Anthony's studio.

The young woman in the office, on getting their names, showed great interest.

"Oh," she said, "I've heard of you. You're the two record-smashers. My! I wish I was as smart as you. If I were I'd be writing books like Bertha Clay — or something. Say, you're to go right up, because Mr. Anthony says your work is to be rushed. This way, boys— right up them stairs. He's got everything ready."

Up the stairs they skipped, Albert in the lead. He realized he was in the presence of Mr. Anthony by bumping full tilt into that distinguished young photographer.

Mr. Anthony was an artist by nature. He showed it in his dress, in his hair, in his actions, and, his intimate friends avowed, in his moods. Mr. Anthony was temperamental.

"I think you've arrived," he said, balancing himself with no little difficulty. "Oh, heavens!" he exclaimed, stepping back and gazing with sheer delight upon Albert's face. "Your features, young man, as I see them, stand for the highest type of Italian beauty."

"Oh, crickey!" cried Albert, breaking into a smile.

"Hey, Rosalind," called the artist, "come up at once." Her name, by the way, was Mary Jane. Rosalind was a free translation made by Mr. Anthony himself.

"Look, Rosalind, look at that face. Can you beat it? It's Little Italy."

"Sakes alive!" said Mary Jane.

"That face, Rosalind," continued Mr. Anthony, staring straight at the blushing boy, is

' "Full of the warm South, Full of the true, the blushful Hippocrene, With beaded bubbles winking at the brim, And purple-stained mouth."

200 HIS LUCKIEST YEAR

Mary Jane gasped, then recovering herself, she put her arms akimbo, and answered:

"That's just what I thought, sir, when I first seen him."

"And this youth," continued the photographer, turning eyes almost as enthusiastic upon Bob, "is another type —the cherubic."

"Thank you, sir," said Bob.

"But you don't look just right, boy. Your eyes are a trifle swollen. You look as if you've been crying. Rosalind, bring this cherub boy to the lavatory, and see that he douches his eyes till they look normal."

"Yes, sir," answered Mary Jane.

"Now, sir," continued Mr. Anthony, addressing Albert, "sit you down in that chair. That's it. Head erect, chin down. What are you frowning about?"

"I ain't," protested Albert.

"You are. And even if you weren't," added Mr. Anthony, getting behind his machine, "even if you weren't, don't do it again."

The smile that overspread Albert's countenance was brought to an end by a loud click.

"What was that, sir?"

"That was you, my boy. I've got you. It was so easy, so wonderful. All great art is easy. If I were to keep you here for a week.

I'd not succeed in getting a better pose. If you've no objection, boy, I'll put a special picture of you in my art exhibit."

"None at all, sir."

"Thank you, and I'll send you a dozen photos with my compliments. I call them photos; they will be portraits. Rosalind! Rosalind!"

"Yes, sir," answered Mary Jane. "He's all ready now, sir." And forth came Mary Jane with Bob. The eyes were no longer swollen; but the light of joy was gone from Bob's face— eclipsed by the cruel words of a foolish tongue.

For fifteen minutes Bob endeavored to pose. Several times the click was heard; but following upon the click came some expression of disgust from the photographer.

"You've got a great face," he observed, "and I ought to get a great picture out of it. When I tell you to look pleasant you try, but you don't succeed.

"Suppose," he said, after taking several turns up and down the room, during which he ran his hands furiously through his hair, "suppose, boy, you try to look serious. Think of something sad."

It was so easy for poor Bob just then to think of something sad. He obeyed at once.

202 HIS LUCKIEST YEAR

"Stop! Stop!" implored the artist. "You look like Romeo at the tomb of Juliet. Hey, Rosalind, Rosalind! Come up at once."

Mary Jane, chewing gum and making no secret of it, presently appeared.

"Rosalind!" exclaimed Mr. Anthony.

"Yes, sir," answered Mary Jane.

"I'm in a peck of trouble, Rosalind."

"You look it, sir," admitted Mary Jane.

"This stout youth has got me in a predicament. I have taken his picture seven times. But each is an ordinary thing. To reproduce any of them would injure my standing as an artist, Rosalind."

"What's the diff ?" queried Mary Jane.

Mr. Anthony fixed an indignant eye upon her.

"You ought to be ashamed of yourself, Rosalind."

"I ain't," retorted Mary Jane.

"Away with idle persiflage!" said Mr. Anthony.

Mary Jane loved big words, and reverenced them. She straightened up, and, for the moment, ceased chewing.

"Rosalind," continued the artist, pulling a single hair from his head, holding it up to the light and staring at it intently, "I've made this boy—this cherubic boy — look pleasant, and it doesn't work right. I know he ought to look pleasant, but I fear he's temperamental, and this isn't his day, Rosalind."

"No," assented Mary Jane, "it isn't his day."

"And I've asked him to look gloomy, and he does the part to perfection. The effect is too tragic."

"I guess," suggested Mary Jane, "that he looks like one of those moving-picture men, like Owen Moore when things don't come his way."

"An excellent criticism, Rosalind." Now, what would you suggest?"

The young lady put her arms akimbo, and, chewing more vigorously than ever, frankly examined Bob's features.

"He has a good heart, he has."

"Yes, Rosalind."

"And I'd say if he were to think of his friends, of the people he loves, you'd get his best face."

"Rosalind, you're a genius!"

"Oh, ain't I the little genius, though?" retorted Mary Jane.

"I think you've got the right idea. Some day, if I can get my courage up to the sticking point, I'm going to propose to you and marry you before I change my mind, Rosalind."

Mary Jane, ceasing to chew, put on the face of a tragedy queen. Giving Mr. Anthony a look of magnificent disdain, she turned on her heels and departed, with movement stately and slow, down the stairway. Albert was by way of being impressed with the young lady's demeanor, but the arms, akimbo, supplemented by a wink which she threw at him as she turned, left him free to conjecture that her feelings were little if at all lacerated.

"That young woman," soliloquized the artist photographer, still pacing the room, "under the homeliest forms of speech, and under a shirt-waist which you can buy at ninety -eight cents in any department store, conceals a heart rich with a sense of beauty. It is true she loves to stand with arms akimbo, it is true she considers the chewing of gum as a sort of public function, it is true-Suddenly his words stopped, and he gasped. With a spring and a bound, he had reached the camera.

"Don't move," he cried. Then there was a click. »i

"I've got you!" he cried. "Oh, but I've got you. Say, my boy, what were you thinking of just then? You looked something like a picture of St. Augustine. You were gazing dreamily into space, your chin resting in your

right palm, and its elbow supported by the other. Say, what were you thinking of?"

Bob blushed.

"Of a dream I had last night."

"It must have been a very, very beautiful dream," said Mr. Anthony.

While the two boys were making their adieu there was an interesting scene in a bank within one square of the studio.

Colonel Robert Bridwell was discussing the news of the day with a real-estate agent, a wholesale grocer, and a lawyer. They were still talking when the bank president entered.

"By the way, Mr. Lawton," cried the colonel, "just fix up my book, will you, and cash my balance."

"What!" cried Lawton, "you're not drawing out?"

"That's what I am," said the colonel. "And the reason is I don't want my money to pass through your hands. You don't look good to me any more."

"Wh-what's the matter?' asked Lawton.

"You are! See here, Lawton, do you know what I've been working for the last six weeks?"

"The orphans' picnic."

"Precisely. I think we ought to work for

the orphans. Poor little kiddies, they have no friends. We all feel sorry for them. We all work for them. All except you."

"What's that?" asked Lawton.

"What about the orphan, Bob Ryan?" asked the colonel.

"Bob Ryan!" repeated Lawton. "I didn't know that he was an orphan."

"Oh, you didn't? Bob Ryan has been helping me for three weeks. He's the cleanest, most energetic boy I've ever met. He's going to help me all day at the picnic on July fourth. He's going to be my aide-de-camp. And you, sir, with your confounded tongue that ought to be thoroughly dry-cleaned after it's been laundered first, have had the meanness to talk about that boy so that, as far as you're concerned, he hasn't a rag of reputation left."

"I didn't say he was an orphan, Colonel."

"I wish you had," returned the colonel, "and had let it go at that. But you did worse. You insinuated that there was something wrong about his parentage. Don't deny it — we've had the story traced up. And if it were true, sir, that there was something wrong about his parentage, he'd be worse off than an orphan, poor fellow. Go on now and fix up my balance. I'll be back in an hour or so, and when

I come I'll leave you a list of streets you'd better avoid if you want to save your precious skin."

And white with anger, the colonel left the bank.

CHAPTER XVI

Bob's picture produces effects which, as the tequel will show, more than atone for his failure. He falls asleep to be awakened by a delightful surprise.

ON the morning of July the fifth the mail carrier who served the good people of Pioneer Street found his work unusually simple. Little boys and girls met him at the threshold of their respective homes, and, seizing the mail from his hands, rushed feverishly indoors. They were all looking for Bob's picture.

Alice O'Shea was the first to get possession of the coveted issue of the Catholic Telegraph. She had stationed herself at the head of the street and there held up the astonished mail carrier. She opened the paper at once and was quick to discover on the inside sheet opposite the editorial page the pictures of a laughing boy full of sunny Italy and of a thoughtful, dreamy-eyed lad, his chin resting in his open palm, who was looking inquiringly into space. The pictures were side by side, and under them were printed the names and addresses of

the two boys, with a statement concerning their wonderfully high percentage in the great contest. Alice gazed intently, gave a shriek of delight, and dashed down the street at full speed to show the wonderful thing to her best friend.

On the way she stopped to greet Brother Cyril, who happened to be coming up the street.

"Oh, look, Brother Cyril," she cried. "Isn't it cute?"

Brother Cyril, on seeing the pictures, gave a start.

"Why," he exclaimed, "they are wonderful photographs. One might call them L'Allegro and Il Penseroso. But I never saw that expression on Bob Ryan's face before. It looks strangely like him, and yet there's an expression on his face such as I never expected to see."

"I think he looks lovely," said Alice.

"It's the face," continued Brother Cyril, "of one in great sorrow. Bob Ryan never knew a sorrow in his life."

"They've been salamandering him," explained Alice.

"What's that?" asked the brother.

"They've been salamandering him," she replied in her most distinct tones. "That's what

my father said. He said some people love to lie about other people, and they've been telling lies about Bob."

"Oh," said the brother, "the scandalmongers have been calumniating him."

"Yes," assented Alice; "that's what I said. They're a lot of salamanders. And," she continued, doubling one fist, rolling her eyes and frowning fiercely, "I wish I was a man. So does Elizabeth. So does Mary Fitzgerald."

"Why?" asked Brother Cyril.

"We'd punch 'em good and hard." Saying which, Alice once more broke into a run, leaving the Brother to conjecture what had given rise to the talk about Bob and why it had brought upon the boy's face that strange, appealing expression.

Brother Cyril was not the only one to be stirred by the unusual photograph. It interested all who saw it. It caused wonder and discussion.

Angelo Corcoran, chancing to enter his employer's office, saw the Telegraph lying open on the desk. The part containing the picture lay exposed. He took it up, gave one look and caught his breath. He looked again.

"My God!" he exclaimed, and left the room as though he had seen a vision.

In a smaller town a lady in mourning saw

the picture. At the first glance she uttered a cry and fell fainting to the floor.

Bob Ryan, seated at his desk, saw the picture, too. He glanced at it and threw it aside with a heavy heart. It brought back keenly to his memory the insult which had so much to do with the sad expression which distinguished his face in the photograph.

Bob had seen Father Carney that very morning and had told him his troubles.

' 'Be thou as chaste as ice, as pure as snow, thou shalt not escape calumny.' Bob, you've had a splendid year, my boy; and you have been a credit to the school. Your influence has been strong and it has all been for good. The Sodality has done wonderful work with you as prefect. But besides all this, you've been too popular. You remember, Bob, at the time of Confirmation, when I advised you to wait another year."

"Yes, Father."

"Somehow I haven't the least doubt but that you were truly and properly baptized. But we could get no record; and we were obliged either to baptize you conditionally or wait. My reason, Bob, for asking you to wait was because I felt quite sure that the mystery surrounding your first years would be cleared up very shortly."

212 HIS LUCKIEST YEAR

"Yes, Father."

"Perhaps I made a mistake. No doubt some busybodies began to inquire why you did not receive Confirmation. It would be just like Lawt —er—just like some people I know to take up a thing like that and make the most of it. All the same, I still believe that after this storm sunshine will come again."

"Thank you, Father. Do you know that my year is up to-day?"

"What year, Bob?"

"I guess you might call it my year of exile. You know, my father made me swear to change my name from Evans to Ryan, and to stay away from Dubuque, my home town, for one year. That happened on last July the fifth."

"And you feel like going back?"

"I certainly do, Father."

Father Carney indulged in a moment's reflection.

"Bob," he said, "I believe it's the best thing you could do. I understand how you feel. Just at present this town is not the place for you. Dangerous tongues have done for you what they have done for the very best men. But mark this, Bob: You'll come back some day in triumph, and your slanderers will be

punished in God's own way. By the by, have you money enough to travel?"

"I was at the Orphans' Picnic yesterday," answered Bob, breaking into a smile, "helping Colonel Bridwell. He's a daisy, ain't he? He went out of his way to make much of me. I'm sure he must have heard the story. Isn't he a daisy, though? Well, I've spent nearly every cent I've got in the world; I haven't much more than will pay my rent for this week, and a few odd bills. But I'm sure I can get some money, Father."

"And so am I," said Father Carney, with unusual cordiality. Praise of Colonel Bridwell, though Bob knew it not, was music to his ears.

"The colonel called me up this morning, and told me what noble work you had done at his picnic department store. He says he noticed that you were short of money toward evening, and that if you need anything I'm to advance you the cash, and he'll fix it up with me later."

"Isn't that kind of him!" exclaimed Bob "Thank you, Father Carney. I'll think about it, and I'll let you know. I don't like traveling on other people's money, but I'm tempted to get away. So many people stare at me and make remarks."

"Bob, are those people the ones you know?"

"No, Father, they were never friends of mine. I just know them by sight—that is, most of them."

"And what about your friends?"

"Oh, they're nicer than ever."

"Then, why worry? In spite of lies and insinuations you haven't lost a friend. Isn't that fine, Bob?"

"Why, yes, Father; I guess it is. I never looked on it in that way before. I ought to be grateful. But there's another thing: I'm so lonesome."

"Lonesome?"

"Yes, Father. I haven't heard a word for ten days or more — nearly two weeks— from Anita or Tom Temple or any of my old friends. And besides, as you probably know, Mrs. Corcoran and my best friend, Albert, went to Iowa the night before last to visit Mrs. Symmes. And I'm just as lonesome as I can be."

Bob returned to his room. The mail carrier, as already set down, left him a copy of the Telegraph, but no letter. Bob fell into a meditation, and from meditation into a sleep. The strenuous work at the picnic, lasting until nearly midnight, had exhausted him.

At the noon hour the landlady peeped in, and retired discreetly on tiptoe, leaving the boy undisturbed.

The afternoon was fast advancing toward sunset, when a loud knock aroused the boy from his slumbers.

"Come in," he cried, jumping to his feet and rubbing his eyes. Then there came from his throat a cry of joy.

"What!" he yelled. "Tom Temple and Lucille Reade?"

"Not on your life," answered Tom genially. "Permit me, Bob: Mr. Thomas Temple—and wife!"

CHAPTER XVII

Showing how brides and grooms should act when children greet them. A last look at the Flower of Pioneer Street. Bob's farewell. Alice and Elizabeth meet the Lady in Black.

BOB started to put his hand under his noble chin; but before he could complete his favorite gesture, Lucille, smiling and blushing, threw her arms about him and planted a kiss upon the spot which his gesture would have covered. Whereupon Tom Temple in turn caught him in a stout embrace and whirled him about the room.

"What! What! Why—how—" blurted Bob.

"That's it exactly," answered Tom to these wild and incoherent exclamations. "You've said it all in words of one syllable." Here Tom whirled Bob into a chair and held him down. "Yes, Bob; it's exactly as you say:

'The voice that breathed o'er Eden,

That earliest wedding day, The primal marriage blessing,

It hath not passed away."

'Bob, delighted, startled, dazed, gazed at Lucille. Lucille, pink as a peony, gazed at Tom Temple. Tom, gurgling, rippling with laughter, returned the gaze, and suddenly threw his arms about Lucille, who, to do her justice, showed a like activity.

"Oh!" exclaimed Bob, bubbling over with joy, "I see!"

"See what?" cried Tom, disengaging himself. "It's about time. Bob, we've gone and got married." After which declaration the happy couple, like mountain torrents, rushed into mutual arms.

"I should think," observed Bob, "it must have happened only a few minutes ago."

"Change the word minutes to hours, Bob. We were staggering up the aisle of a church — at least I was staggering—at five o'clock this morning, to an air from Lohengrin; and we were duly married; and we took forthwith the first train, to speed to you, our best friend. For it is you who are the author of our present bliss."

"Good gracious!" gasped the delighted boy. "How do I come in?"

"Your letters to me about Lucille, when you first saw her, put me in love with her unseen."

"And your description of Tom Temple*

Bob," continued Lucille, "had the same wondrous effect on me."

"Dan Cupid," continued Tom, "must have loaned you two of his darts; and your marksmanship was perfect."

"And we're not only in love with each other," added Lucille, "but we're also in love with you, dear Bob."

"And our wedding journey," Tom went on, "would be incomplete without you."

"Wedding journey!" Bob echoed.

"Yes, wedding journey. We've sped hither to get you. There's a train leaves in two hours. So pack up and off we go."

"This — this is so sudden!" said Bob, wondering whether he was really awake.

"That's what Lucille said when I laid my heart at her feet."

"I didn't, and you didn't," protested Lucille.

"Well, your words were to that effect, and my actions came to what I just said. Bob, when Lucille and I met each other for the first time, everything else was off. Everything you said of Lucille was less than true. From that hour I went about like Orlando in the forest or Arden. The birds sang, and their song was Lucille; the brooks murmured Lucille; and when I sat me down to write an

ode or a sonnet my pen wrote nothing but Lucille."

"Some of your best poems," objected Bob, "have come out in the last six weeks."

"Oh, they weren't mine," answered the radiant poet. "I looked simply into Lucille's eyes and wrote. Result

All the buds and bells of May From dewy sward or thorny spray.

Or I looked into her heart, and if my verses were poor it was because the beauty I saw there was 'too pure for the touch of a word.'"

"But how did you get here so soon after your marriage?" Bob asked.

"We were not married at Lucille's home. We came south, to a town in Indiana, where I have a friend who happens to be a great priest," answered Tom. "You see, there were reasons for a quiet wedding, too."

"But what's become of Anita and Tom Reade? I haven't heard a word from them."

"No wonder," answered Lucille. "Anita was flower girl, and she's been too busy and excited to write. My brother Tom has been in charge of arrangements, and has had no time for anything else."

"And moreover," added Tom Temple, "the

eager-eyed Anita was so afraid she'd let out the secret of July fifth — our wedding. Strange, Bob, I didn't think of it when we named the day; yet it's the very anniversary of the day your father issued the edict of your exile."

"Yes, Tom; and I'm free again, free to return to Dubuque, free to take up my own name."

"Don't I know it?" said the poet. "And that's why you're coming with us to Dubuque. Bob, we're going to find out everything; and, till we do, you are our Bob."

"What's that?" asked the boy.

"We're going to adopt you."

"Oh, go on," said Bob, half in laughter, half in tears.

"Well, anyhow, we'll keep you to be held until called for."

"Ohl" cried Lucille, who had gone to one of the windows looking out on the street, "did you ever see such beautiful children?"

Tom and Bob rushed over to the window, and shared with Lucille in a sight which was enough to bring joy to any lover of childhood.

Gathered about the automobile which had conveyed the happy pair to Pioneer Street was the flower of the neighborhood, boys and girls

in their best attire. No sooner had the machine stopped before Bob's room than Johnny O'Brien, first taking note of the handsome young man and stately beauty who issued from it, sped from house to house with the glowing news that Bob Ryan was receiving automobile friends and that something important was to happen. Every house on the street blessed with boy or girl forthwith became a scene of activity; with the result that in a few minutes gay Alice and laughing Elizabeth, and Marian and Margaret Hunter—in a word, all the youth and beauty of the street—were assembled, forming a riot of color around the touring car. How they rejoiced over it! That car, they reasoned with the imaginative logic of childhood, was enough to rehabilitate Bob in the eyes of all his "salamanders."

"Look," cried quick-eyed Johnny O'Brien, "look at Bob's window."

"Look," cried Bob from above, "aren't they a nice set, though? They're all friends of mine."

"Hello, Bob!" cried fifty voices as one, as at young O'Brien's words fifty smiling and cordial faces turned upward toward his window.

"Hello, boys and girls!"

"I say," cried Tom Temple, "this is too

much for me. You think I'll stand here and see such friends—such wonderful boys and girls—and not shake hands with 'em?" And Tom, catching Lucille with one arm and Bob with the other, made hastily for the stairway.

"Hello, boys and girls!" said Tom as they reached the front stoop.

"How do you do, sir?" responded Alice, and those few who were not overawed by the vision.

"I understand that you are all friends of our Bob."

"You bet your boots 1" cried Johnny O'Brien, speaking for all.

"Well, he's the best friend I ever had," added Lucille.

"They've both just been married," said Bob, smiling in his old way. "Did you ever see a lovelier couple?"

Screams and shouts of joy rent the air. Alice rushed to Lucille's side, and that sweet young bride caught up the child and hugged her. Then Lucille was surrounded. Every girl on Pioneer and in the environs thereof pushed and struggled to be kiesed by the blushing beauty—every girl and most of the very small boys.

When, after the excitement had died down, Tom Temple asked the multitude whether they liked ice cream and had received an earnest and fervent answer in the affirmative from the tots of the assemblage, the chauffeur was commissioned to get two gallons from the nearest place; and, as Alice and Elizabeth kindly consented to enter the machine and show him the way, there was sure to be no serious delay.

It was just then that Mr. Lawton, turning from Pike into Pioneer, came into view. On seeing the gay and happy throng, with Bob the j oiliest and most prominent of all, he was minded to turn back and seek some more circuitous way to his lodging house. He hesitated, faltered, turned half-way round, then compromised by crossing to the other side of the street. Nothing of all this escaped the watchful eye of Johnny O'Brien, and as the unhappy man came opposite the festive bridal party, Master Johnny, the dead-game sport, shrieked out at the top of his voice

"Three cheers for Bob Ryan."

And it was Tom Temple who led the cheer? ing—cheering the like of which was never before heard in that vicinity.

"Ha!" said Johnny darkly to Alice's brother, "I guess that finishes him all right. Did you see his head go down?"

While the children were discussing the ice

cream, Tom announced that he was going to take Bob away.

"For good? Oh, not for good!" implored Alice.

"He'll see you all again, children. In an hour or so we start for his home town, Du-buque."

It is to the credit of Alice and Johnny O'Brien that they ate no more ice cream that evening. Leaving their dishes unfinished, they entered into a secret conference —a thing not without its difficulties, as everybody of consequence in that juvenile party came up to know what it was all about.

"Go away," said Alice.

"Make a noise like a hoop and roll along," said Johnny to each and every one.

Presently the two revealed their discussion in low tones to their curious friends;

whereupon there was a quick scurrying to homes, and Pioneer Street was once more deserted.

Aided by the skilled hands of Lucille, and embarrassed by the bungling efforts of Tom Temple, Bob, within an hour's time, having packed, put his room in order, attended to the payment of outstanding debts, passed out from the place dear to him by a thousand and one beautiful associations. He left it regretfully

but bravely, little knowing that it was to be his room no more.

Outside all was quiet. Not a soul could be seen save the chauffeur, wearing upon his stolid features an expression too solemn to be natural. Then, as the three stepped toward the auto, suddenly from nook and corner and cranny and doorway sprang forth with shout and scream the entire juvenile population of the street, with numerous friends from the neighborhood.

"Surprise! Surprise!" piped the girls.

"Hurrah!" yelled the boys.

Then Alice and Johnny O'Brien stepped forth, holding between them a bouquet of American Beauties.

"Mr. and Mrs. Thomas Tentacle," said Alice, "we wish you a happy wedding journey, with lots more of them."

"And many happy returns," added Johnny O'Brien. "And these roses are red and beautiful, Mrs. Temple, and they're for you. But they're not in it with your cheeks."

Tom Temple, for the first and only time in this history, was speechless. Lucille, speechless, too, looked as though a beautiful sunset afterglow had passed into her face.

Then came Bob's turn. Each and every

child approaching him handed him a flower, saying:

"Good-by, Bob."

There was an embarrassment of flowers; so much that Tom and Lucille and the chauffeur were obliged to come to Bob's assistance.

"Good-by, boys and girls," said Bob hoarsely, taking the last flower and placing it in his buttonhole.

"Good-by, good-by," cried the children.

"God forgive me," said Bob a minute later, as the machine turned on Fourth Street. He was the first to break the silence.

"Why, Bob, what's the matter?"

"Oh, for a week or so I've been blue and discontented. And why? Because people I don't really know were saying unkind things about me. How silly I wasl Let them talk all they like. Just look at my friends 1"

Half an hour later, as daylight and the night were merging, there dashed up to Bob's residence another automobile, from which alighted a portly gentleman, classical of feature, and a lady clothed in black.

Alice and Elizabeth, gently mourning, were seated, as it were on guard, at the entrance to the house.

?° id the gentleman, in a deep

voice, "but could either of you young ladies tell me whether Robert Ryan is in?"

The two young ladies jumped to their feet.

"Please, sir," said Alice, "he's just gone."

"What! Gone?" cried the lady, in the sweetest and saddest accents Alice had ever heard.

"My dear lady," said the man, "I entreat you to be calm. Just leave it to me. You say he's gone, young miss?"

"Yes, sir; he went off in an automobile just about half an hour ago," answered Alice.

"And where, may I ask, has he gone to?"

"He went with the nicest man and lady, who were just married, to Dubuque."

"Oh!" cried the lady.

"And," continued Alice, "I'm afraid they're taking him away for good. And Bob Ryan was the nicest boy I ever saw."

The lady suddenly bent down and kissed Alice, and then took out her handkerchief and wept. Whereupon Alice wept, too, and Elizabeth, much affected and not to be outdone, lifted up her voice in grief. As for the gentleman, he looked as awkward and as helpless as any diplomat in such circumstances.

"My dear lady," he said, after tugging helplessly at his moustache, "I beg you not to be cast down. Perhaps we may catch him at the station if we hurry."

"It's g-g-g-gone," sputtered Alice.

"What's gone?" asked the man.

"The t-t-train. Johnny O'Brien sneaked down to see, and he telephoned over fifteen minutes ago that B-Bob was smiling back at him as the c-cars pulled out."

And as Alice resumed her weeping the man helped the lady in black into the machine.

CHAPTER XVIII

Tom Temple turns back time in his flight. Old faces and old friends once more.

"T THOUGHT we were going to Dubuque," JL said Bob early next morning.

The train had come to a stop at an obscure Iowa town, and Tom and Lucille were gathering up their belongings.

"So we are, O cherub of Iowa; but there's more than one way of going there. Get hold of your things, Bob."

Awaiting them outside was a touring car.

"Oh!" cried Bob. "I think I see now. We're going to travel in this machine."

"Right-o. Jump in. You think you see; but you don't."

For many golden minutes Lucille, fresh as a flower dew-sprinkled and in early blossom, and Tom, running over with animal spirits, vied with each other in entertaining the happy boy. How a few hours had changed him! All his troubles were gone—driven utterly away by the advent of love.

It was only when the automobile came to a stop that the conversation ceased. Bob looked about him, took a deep breath, and cried:

"Why! If this doesn't look like old times! Say, Lucille, pinch me; I must be dreaming. Surely, I know this spot."

Before him, placid, broad, grand, dimpling in the sun, lay the Mississippi river.

"Jump out, Bob," ordered Tom. "We'll take a walk down to the bank. Here, Lucille, you take care of him while I speak to the chauffeur."

"This river is dear to me," said Lucille, holding Bob's hand, as the two walked down toward the bank.

"It was somewhere about here," said Bob, "that I met Matt Morris, one of my best friends. It is clear to me."

"It was on these banks," said Lucille, "that I met you."

"Thank you, Lucille. And it was on this river that I motored the best boat a boy could have. It was on this river that I had that wonderful picnic, and I bade Mrs. Symmes good-by, and she gave me the best dog in the world."

"And it was on these banks, these bonny

banks," continued Lucille, "that Tom and j »»

Here Lucille stopped and blushed into a new phase of beauty.

"I know what you mean," said Bob. "It was on these banks that you named the day."

Lucille's silvery laugh was yet ringing on the magic air of the golden morning, when, skirting a growth of bushes, Bob saw a sight which brought his hand to his eyes.

"My goodness me!" he cried, after another look. "It's The Wanderer"

"Exactly," said Tom, catching up with them, "the happy Wanderer, at your service, Bob, as long as you want it."

"What—what—does this mean?" asked Bob.

"It seems, O cherub of Iowa," said Tom, clapping Bob on the back, "that we're going to turn Time back in his flight. Jump aboard, young man, and convey us to the sylvan abode of the woodland Apollo known to mortals as Matt Morris."

It was a happy pilot who sent The Wanderer spinning down the river. In a few moments they touched land. Bob's eyes danced as in a glance he picked out the old canoe, hidden in the old place. It seemed incredible that nearly a year had passed since he last saw it.

"Oh, but this looks good!" exclaimed the boy, jumping out of the boat. "That canoe makes me feel certain that Matt's here again."

"Right you are, Bob!" And Matt Morris, taller, bigger, finer than ever, sprang from be-

232 HIS LUCKIEST YEAR

hind a tree and threw himself upon his old mate.

The violence of their welcome merged into a friendly wrestling contest, in which Bob, to Matt's supreme joy, held his own perfectly.

"Excuse me," Matt said, turning to Lucille, "but Bob and I just naturally mix it up whenever we meet. I'm so glad to meet you again. How do you do, Mr. Temple?"

"If I did like you," returned the poet, "I'd go to a hospital for repairs. The strenuous life is certainly yours."

"That's the way Bob and I used to carry on, day in, day out. Say, Bob, you're stronger than ever. My, what a player you'd make for our team —even now, though you're not quite fifteen! Oh, how I wish you could come to Campion College I"

"And maybe I don't wish it either," returned Bob. "I'm in love with Campion the way Tom was in love with Lucille, and the way Lucille was in love with Tom."

"What's the answer?" queried Matt.

"They loved each other before they met. I've never seen Campion ; but I have heard of it. And you're there, and Tom Reade, one of the nicest boys in the world, is there."

"Not much," said a new voice; "he's right here, and on the job." And Tom Reade himself, dashing down the steep ascent, landed, before Bob could turn, squarely upon that robust youth's shoulders.

"And what," asked the beaming Bob, after the first excitement of greeting had passed, "brings you here?"

"Matt and I are partners this summer, Bob; and I beg to announce that breakfast is served. Follow me." And Tom, holding Bob's hand, dashed up the ascent.

The eager Bob was anything but loath to be thus laid captive. Even Tom and Lucille, entering into the spirit of the place, trotted after the leader. It was a breathless crowd that seated themselves at the improvised table in Matt's sylvan retreat. The cooking, excellent as it was, could not compare with the appetites upon which it waited. Tom Temple, toward the conclusion of the meal, declared that it was the greatest wedding breakfast in song or story.

Toward the close of this never-to-be-forgotten breakfast Tom Reade, trying to attract as little attention as possible, slipped back into the cave. After a few seconds he appeared once more, and cried out:

"Say, Bob, what was the name of that dog of yours?"

"Hobo," shouted Bob.

At the word, out from the cave sprang a shining-eyed dog. Bob's hands relaxed, and from them a plate dropped upon the stone floor and broke into fragments.

"Hobo!" he cried once more; and at the word the dog ran to him and raised eyes of tender inquiry.

"It's Hobo the Second," exclaimed Tom Reade. "It took me a week to discover him. He's a blood relative of your dog, Bob, and as like him, almost, as it's possible for one dog to resemble another."

"And it's your dog, Bob," said Matt. "It's our present."

"By George!" exclaimed Bob, having secured in a few seconds Hobo's undying love, "this thing is all like a dream."

"It's more like 'when dreams come true,'" corrected Tom Temple, darting an ardent glance at Lucille.

"I wish," said Tom Reade, "that you people would cut out the sentiment stuff and help clean up."

"That's right," said Matt, "we start in fifteen minutes."

"What's that?" asked Bob.

"Never you mind, Bob Ryan, just get ready."

And twenty minutes later they were aboard

The Wanderer —the wedding pair, Tom Reade, Matt Morris, Bob Ryan, and Hobo II. They landed presently at another familiar spot, and proceeded to visit the little church where Bob had made his first Communion. The visit was short but fervent, and the prayer of all was a prayer of thanksgiving.

Up the river they pursued their happy way. At noon time they reached a little town, where at an inn there awaited them a dainty lunch, but, as Bob and the two boys with perfect justice considered, a very light one.

The touring car was there, too. Everything, Bob could not but observe, had been prearranged. Over hill and dale they went at top speed. At top speed, too, went the hours. It was a continuous carnival of joy.

About four o'clock, however, the younger members of the party, Bob, Tom Reade, and Matt, began to look a trifle uneasy.

"What's the matter, boys?" asked Lucille.

"Oh, nothing," answered Matt.

"Nothing," echoed Tom Reade. "I wouldn't say nothing myself, but that's what my stomach is saying."

"That lunch we took," added Bob, "was very nice indeed; but it was rather light."

"How long can you hold out, Bob?" asked the poet.

"Oh, I guess I can stand it, Tom, as long as you like."

"For such a lovely couple," observed Tom Reade, looking severely at Lucille, "I'm willing to starve."

"Halloa!" cried Bob, jumping up and gazing intently ahead, "as sure as my name's Bob, if that isn't the Blue Bird Inn!"

Even as he spoke the machine drew up before the quaint old hostelry.

Then out came, screaming, Anita, leaping up and down like a jumping-jack. She threw herself upon Bob and gave him a welcome more easily imagined than described. And before Bob was quite finished with paying his respects to the ardent young lady forth came Mrs. Corcoran, her laugh ringing birdlike in the air, and Albert, his face running over with smiles and glowing with the "warm South." Close behind these two followed mine host and his amiable wife; and then, to complete the party, Mr. and Mrs. Reade with their happy children. A perfect storm of greeting ensued—hugging, hand-shaking, laughter, and what not, in which all took an active part save Masters Tom Reade and Matt Morris. These young gentlemen were properly disgusted, and Tom made no secret of it.

"I say," he said, snatching Lucille bodily

from the embrace of Mrs. Symmes, "are we to starve to death while you people act like a lot of howling hyenas on parade?"

Mrs. Symmes, breaking into a laugh—a laugh the twin of her newly found sister's—clapped her hands and cried:

"Dinner's served."

Tom Reade and Matt Morris rushed for the house.

It was then that the boys understood the reason of the light lunch. A banquet was awaiting them, a banquet prepared by Mrs. Symmes and Mrs. Corcoran, the two most wonderful cooks, Tom Temple averred, since the days of Lucullus.

"Do you know," said Bob to Anita, "that I believe this has been the happiest day of my life?"

"It's been mine, too, Bob," said Anita. "Bob, are you going to stay with me always?"

Bob laughed. He was about to frame a reply when Tom Temple announced:

"Let everybody get ready. In fifteen minutes we take a boat ride on the river."

"Goodness gracious, Anita!" said Bob, "what's next? I'm getting dizzy."

"It's a secret, Bob," Anita made answer. "And did you miss my letters, Bob?"

"I should say I did. The loss of them made me blue."

"I'm just tickled to know that," said Anita.

Once more The Wanderer, brought up the river by a motor truck, was awaiting them, and into it, by some miracle of squeezing and contriving, entered the entire Reade family, Tom Temple, Matt Morris, Albert Corcoran and mother, Mr. and Mrs. John Symmes, Bob Ryan, and, of course, Hobo II.

It was nearing sunset. The water, the air, the woodlands, the singing birds, all united to make this hour what Bob described as the close of a perfect day. But justice compels me to state that these meaner beauties were lost sight of in the intercourse of love and laughter and news of this chosen party. Indeed, there was talk and laughter a plenty, talk and laughter and song, in which the praises of Campion College, you may be sure, were not overlooked by that promising singer, Matt Morris. In the rich afterglow of a flawless sunset, Bob Ryan, retiring, as it were, into his own heart, fell into a meditation of pure thankfulness, when Anita's caressing hand upon his shoulder aroused him.

"Look, Bob," she said. "Over there. Don't you know it?"

Bob followed her gesture, and gave a cry

of joy, as he steered the vessel toward the shore, where, neatly shaved and dressed in a store suit, stood a smiling old man; and, enveloped in a cloak which gave her the appearance of Mother Hubbard, with hands reaching out toward him, his ancient wife—Mr. and Mrs, Moss,

CHAPTER XIX

In which one surprise follows upon another.

'' T T EY !" roared the ancient of the river bank,

* * removing his hat and bowing low, "Mistaire Bob. How you do?"

Bob caught the venerable and horny right hand and shook it up and down until the aged consort, sweeping Mose aside with a backhand gesture which nearly cost her the loss of her cloak, took her turn at greeting. And while Mrs. Mose made a carefully prepared speech about the prodigal son's return and there being a glut of fatted calves to celebrate with, Mose bowed and beamed upon each and every member of the party.

"Where's Tom Temple going?" asked Bob, noticing that Tom had got into the touring car.

"If he wanted you to know," returned the old lady, "he'd have told you. Isn't he the gay groom, though? Mose and I consider him the most wonderful young man. Mose says he's the greatest poet living."

"You don't say!" exclaimed the boy. "Have you read some of Tom's poems to Mose?"

"I have not," returned the venerable blue-eyed lady. "And no one else has. But Mose says he can tell by the looks of him that Tom is the greatest living poet. And Mose," she added in a tone of conviction, "is right."

"You've read some of his poems, then?"

"I have not, Bob. I don't go in for poetry. But I'm old enough to tell a poet when I see one."

"Anna," said Mose, "you go up by the house and see to the lemonade, while I talk to Bob. Hey, Bob," he went on as the old woman, not without visible signs of reluctance, made for the ancient hut, "I am ver' glad to see you— oh, so glad, Bob"—here the massive right forefinger came into play—"I tell you something. From the day you leave till this day you return I pray for you eve'y nide. I never forget. I pray for you—so." The venerable man raised his big eyes toward the heavens, folding at the same time his big hands. "And Anna, she pray, too. And we pray for Tom Temple, too—Tom the great poeter."

"Thank you," returned Bob. "Do you know all these people?"

"Bob, I no lie to you. These people, your friends, they my friends, too. If I no treat them right—God Almighty, He punish me, the way He punish the widow woman when the

242 HIS LUCKIEST YEAR

widow he tole a lie to God Almighty. He turn the widow woman's boy into a tombear."

Around Bob and Mose all had now gathered; and Bob introduced Mose by name to every one present.

"Ladies and gentlemen," said Mose, when he had bowed profoundly to each, "I tell you somet'ing. I now eighty-five year old, and my wife—

"Here, Mose, you let me out."

"My wife, he older than me."

"Her ears are thirty years younger," snapped the old lady.

"And now," Mose went on, "I weak in my legs, becos they is roomatiz. But when I young, I was the strongest man from Davenport to Dubuque."

"He looks strong yet," observed Matt Morris critically. "Just observe his shoulders and that neck of his."

"Ladies and gentlemen," continued the ancient, throwing his hat away that he might gesticulate more freely. "I no lie to you—I tell you the troot—I neider read nor write."

Mose then went on to give a faithful but incoherent account of his life, his wife at times supplying caustic footnotes.

While the old man, beaming with benevolence, discoursed simply of his former deeds, there was a great stir and bustle about his house higher up on the bank. Several men, genii, it may be, brought together by the Aladdin of the occasion, Mr. Tom Temple, were stringing ropes from tree to tree.

Whether by accident or design, old Mose, standing at the river's edge, held the eyes of the assemblage to such purpose that none of them was aware of those swift workers. Mose Was of interest to all. His stories were good, his idioms were curious, and his gestures and intonation were enough to give new ideas to professional elocutionists.

It was fast growing dark, and the very younger set were fast growing thirsty.

Anita whispered to Bob, "Say, Bob, didn't you hear something about lemonade?"

"I'm pretty thirsty myself," answered Bob.

Anita turned, pulling Bob with her.

"Oh!" cried Bob.

Anita screamed.

The home of Mose was hung about with a profusion of Japanese lanterns.

At Anita's scream all turned and wondered.

"A belated Fourth of July, fair friends," cried Tom Temple, standing at the door of the illuminated hut.

At the words a rocket shot into the air; a

244 HIS LUCKIEST YEAR

giant pinwheel, fastened to one of the trees, spun and sputtered into flaming loveliness; Roman candles, held by unknown hands, spurted out balls, yellow, green, glorious, golden, and for fully a quarter of an hour the night was made splendid.

•"One word, ladies and gentlemen," said Tom, approaching them at the close of the pyrotechnics. "For the past twenty-four hours I've not been quite certain whether it was I who got married or Bob Ryan. By right Lucille ought to be the shining mark, and I ought to come a distant second. But it's not so at all. Everything is Bob Ryan. Everybody's glad to see him. As for Lucille and myself, one would think we'd been married for twenty years. To be serious, it has been my dream for many a moon to return to the old places made dear to me by their associations with that part of my speckled career which led to my meeting my best friend and the finest, the loveliest, lady in the land. My new life began here in the home of honest Mose and his wife. It was here that I lost Bob and found myself. And I have brought all Bob's friends—and may I say mine, too?—together here, that we, Bob and I, may fight our battles o'er and tell how fields are won."

Tom paused, took out his handkerchief, and wiped his heated brow. As the applause subsided, the sound of an automobile as it swept up to the house of Mose brought all to fresh attention.

"Do you think it's another surprise?" Anita asked Bob, as a man jumped from the machine and helped a woman to alight.

"I shouldn't wonder," answered Bob. "This day is so full of surprises, though, that I'm getting hardened to them."

The man, a portly gentleman, dignified in gait, although his walk was brisk, was advancing toward the party as Bob spoke.

"Ladies and gentlemen," he said, removing his hat and bowing with Old-World courtesy, "I beg pardon for intruding on what I clearly see is a gathering of friends, but I have a question to ask which I think so important that it can not be deferred. Is there a young gentleman here answering to the name of Bob Ryan?"

Amidst a chorus of puzzled assents Anita, holding Bob by the hand, stepped forward.

"Sir," she said, "I want to introduce to you my best, my bestest friend—Bob Ryan."

The man shook Bob's hand warmly and deferentially.

"Bob Ryan," he said, "I want you to come with me and to ask you a few questions of a

strictly private nature, the answers to which, truthfully given, can not hurt you in the least and may prove to be most extraordinarily to your advantage. Ladies and gentlemen, will you kindly excuse Bob for a few minutes?"

An extraordinary change had come upon the assembled party. The atmosphere seemed surcharged with some great secret. Something strange was about to happen. As Bob walked off with the strange man all eyes followed the boy.

Half-way up the slope leading to Mose's house the man halted Bob and held him with a whispered dialogue. The man became very nervous and excited. He began presently to rub his hands, and bending down to glance at the boy's face, as though he would read his soul. Finally he took Bob's hand, and made a sign toward the woman, who had remained standing near the auto.

The friends of Bob, several of them catching their breath, looked on in absorbed silence.

At the man's signal the lady hastened toward Bob.

"Now, ma'am," they heard him say, "be calm. You must be calm. I don't think there can be any mistake, but— here, let me ask him a few questions in your presence."

Under the light of the lanterns, which

brought out the faces of Bob and his two interrogators, ensued a scene which none who saw it on that eventful night will ever forget.

The man stood in the center, holding Bob with one hand, the woman with the other. A great wonder was on Bob's face, an overmastering anxiety on the woman's, on the man's an air of absorbing excitement. He appeared to be asking Bob questions. Several times Bob nodded his head in assent. Then the man paused—the beads of sweat dropping from his face—held up his hand, and apparently asking Bob to do the same. It was evident to all that Bob was testifying on oath. As Bob dropped his hand the woman addressed him. Bob opened his mouth, uttered one word, and then

The man released their hands and pulled out his handkerchief; the woman .gave a cry of exquisite joy; and Bob, his face irradiated, threw his arms about her.

As they thus stood, the man, rubbing his eyes and turning toward the transfixed party, exclaimed in a broken voice:

"It's his mother!"

In which the mystery of Bob's childhood is cleared up, and he enters upon a new life.

THE announcement sent a thrill of awe through the listeners. Incoherent ejaculations, low murmurs, and all manner of exclamations gradually merged into expressions of pure joy. Then suddenly from the crowd burst the great-souled Anita and, darting straight at Bob and his mother, cried as she sped:

"Mrs. Ryan, if you're Bob's mother you must kiss me, too."

Fast after the flying Anita bounded Hobo II, and as the lady disengaged herself from Bob and threw her arms about the girl, the dog, barking and jumping, circled about the three in an ecstasy of delight.

Then Bob, holding his mother's hand, with Anita clinging to both, walked toward the group.

"Do you know, mother," he whispered, "that we met once?"

"Indeed I do, Robert. You were the boy that picked up my package as I seated myself in a car."

248

"And I knew you at once when I saw you, mother; but I didn't suspect that I was your son. I knew you as the Lady in Black. Say," he cried, raising his voice, "this is my dear mother, Mrs. Marion Leslie."

"God bless you all," said Mrs. Leslie. "For years I have been grieving for my motherless boy. But I know now that God has given him loving hearts to take my place."

"And this," said Mrs. Leslie's escort, catching Bob by the shoulders, "is Robert Leslie, the only son of Mrs. Marion Leslie. Permit me also to introduce myself. I am Thomas Coleman, Mrs. Leslie's personal friend and attorney."

"But what about that father of Bob's?" asked Tom Temple, after the lawyer and hifr sweet client had shaken hands with each and every one, "the fellow who threw him out into the world."

"That was not his father," said Mr. Cole' man.

"Good!" cried Tom. "I'm glad to hear it."

"Suppose," continued Mr. Coleman, "that we all come up to the immediate premises of our friend Mose, and while Robert Leslie and his mother have a heart-to-heart talk I will tell you their story."

It took little time to follow the lawyer's

250 HIS LUCKIEST YEAR

suggestion. Mr. Coleman had held many a jury in the hollow of his hand, but never in all his experience had he so attentive an audience as the one now before him.

"Some sixteen or seventeen years ago," he began, "there lived in a small Ohio village a lovely young girl—educated in a convent school and of a most winning personality. Her parents were apparently in good circumstances. When at the age of eighteen the girl was graduated from the convent school in Cincinnati, she returned home just in time to take up the duties of the household, for her mother went into a swift decline, and after her death the father lost all interest in his business. Very soon he broke down, and shortly followed his wife — leaving the girl penniless.

"Then John R. Leslie, a young lawyer of great promise, to whom she had been engaged, insisted on a private marriage almost at once. Mr. Leslie, born out of the Catholic Church, had been induced by the girl to study the Catholic teachings. God gave him the faith and he was baptized on the day of their marriage. Mr. Leslie's parents, on learning that their son and heir had embraced the Catholic faith, were furious. They forbade him their house and refused to recognize him as their son. In ronsequence, the young couple, being resolved

to make their own way, left for another part of the State, where Mr. Leslie hung out his shingle and contrived to make just enough to support his wife.

"In course of time there was born to them a son and heir—Robert Leslie. In the eyes of his mother and father he was the finest baby in the world. Judging from what little I have seen of him," added the lawyer, with a smile, "I believe they were right."

"They were, absolutely," said Tom Temple.

"Their married life, hitherto an ideal one," continued the lawyer, "was now a thing of bliss. The father, a big, hearty, whole-souled man, who, by the way, was built very much on the lines of Bob, could never bring himself to believe that his parents would not relent. He felt that he and his wife were undergoing a temporary exile. He sent them a letter giving an account of young Bob, aged seven days. The letter came back unopened.

"Mr. Leslie did not lose courage. He was mystified at the conduct of his parents, and said that they would surely forget and forgive in a year. Before a year had passed the brave young fellow, in attempting to rescue a drowning child—an attempt in which he succeeded— lost his life.

"As I have said, he was a very good lawyer.

252 HIS LUCKIEST YEAR

Now, gentlemen of the—oh, I beg your pardon!—Now, my friends, a good lawyer is a man who can attend in the most wonderful way to other people's business; but just as likely as not he is a baby in taking care of his own. So it came to pass that he died without any insurance on his life or anything in the bank beyond enough money to cover the funeral expenses and pay his outstanding debts. Poor Mrs. Leslie— I hope, by the way, she's not listening—

"You needn't worry," said Tom, "Bob and his mother—and the dog—are walking on the road Bob traversed with me one year ago."

"Very good. As I was saying, poor Mrs. Leslie, who knew less about business than most young wives, was at her wits' end. She wrote a pitiful letter to her husband's people. That letter, with its black-bordered envelope, came back unopened. In the light of what we have since learned it is much to be regretted that she did not take the train and visit these people personally. For her husband was absolutely right. The old people were ready and willing and waiting to forget and forgive."

"How about those returned letters, then?" asked Mr. Reade.

"The question," returned Mr. Coleman, judicially, "is eminently fair and in order. The fact is that the old people never saw those

letters. There lived with them a spinster, their nearest of kin after their son. This gentle creature, with an inquisitiveness which we wonder at without admiring in certain women, inspected every piece of mail that came into the house. It was to her interest to prevent reconciliation; and she certainly put her mind to it. She saw to it that these letters did not go beyond the threshold.

"Mrs. Leslie, then, timid, shrinking, tried to earn a living with the needle for herself and her six-months-old child; for nearly a year she dragged out a precarious existence. Toward the end of that year there came into her life a certain hatchet-faced young man, Thomas Evans by name, who apparently did everything to help her. He got her work, he showed her all manner of kindness; and he proposed. He made his proposal, as they say, at the psychological moment. It was when work was slack, times hard, and the child was showing unfavorable symptoms, resulting, as the mother thought, from insufficient nourishment.

"Almost in despair, she consented. They were to be married privately by a priest, in a village some thirty miles distant. On the appointed day, and arrived at the appointed place, Mrs. Leslie was brought before a squire. But Evans, a bitter bigot, though he had kept this side of him from her, had reckoned with-

out his host. She became indignant. She reminded him of his promise to secure a Catholic priest for the ceremony.

"Then Evans, losing his temper, said such things about her Church as opened her eyes. She declared that under no circumstances could she think of marrying such a man. Upon this Evans, in a towering rage, getting into the machine which had conveyed them thither, left her to get home as best she might.

"She had no money. She attempted to walk home, and was picked up on the road unconscious and brought to a hospital, where for months she struggled for her life. When she left the hospital she succeeded in getting home, only to learn that Evans had disappeared with the child on the day of the proposed wedding.

"And what could she do? The daily papers might have helped her; but news four months old is no news. Money she had none. Moreover, she was temporarily broken in spirit. So she prayed and hoped and worked and wept. Her life was a life of sorrow.

"A little over a year ago Mrs. Leslie was suddenly summoned to the home of her dead husband's mother. She went at once, and was brought to the bedside of the dying woman, whose husband had died three years before. The old woman was sorely repentant. She got

Mrs. Leslie's story, obtained Mrs. Leslie's forgiveness, then summoned her lawyer and made a new will.

"I was the lawyer," said Mr. Coleman, relaxing into a smile. "And I shed no tears when old Mrs. Leslie left one bare dollar to that spinster sister of hers who had intercepted the letters. To Mrs. Leslie, Bob's mother, the old lady left an income of six thousand a year, and to Bob, with his mother as executor, an estate valued at nearly a quarter of a million."

"How much is that?" asked Mose, "enough to support him?"

"Enough to support him," answered the lawyer, "and to help old friends like Mose and his wife to be comfortable for life."

"I tell you something, sir, and I lie not to you. I always tole my wife Anna we will not go to the poorhouse."

"And you were right, Mose. To continue: The old lady, having made her will, very shortly afterward died; and I, who had known Mr. and Mrs. Leslie before their marriage, took up Bob's case. Of course the thing got into the papers, almost before we put detectives on the trail. On the morning of July fifth, just a year ago and a day, we traced Evans as far as Dubuque. In fact, two of our men came to

the house, and just as they made sure that they had trailed the right man Evans and the boy disappeared."

"But why did Evans hold the boy kidnaped all these years?" asked Tom.

"So far as I can make out," answered Mr. Coleman, "he counted on the death of the mother. She was thought to be dying when he stole the boy. He knew the Leslie family, and he knew that they were ready to forgive. Bob would inherit a fortune. That, I believe, is the reason why he tried to marry young Mrs. Leslie."

"I think/' said Tom Temple, "that I can finish the story. When Evans abandoned Bob in the woodlands I discovered the young cherub. It was the finest discovery I ever made. I really thought at the time that I was entertaining a young cherub; I didn't know that it was only a young heir. Of course, your detectives, not knowing that Evans and Bob had parted company, got on the wrong trail. They followed me, they found me in the hospital, and concluded they had been on a false scent, and so started off on some other trail, while Bob, as a member of the Reade family, slipped into Cincinnati. But how in the long run did you discover Bob?"

"Mrs. Leslie," replied the lawyer, "made the discovery herself. It was that picture in the Catholic Telegraph, a picture, by the way, which would never have appeared had it not been for Bob's failure to come out first in the contest. It was a lucky failure.

"When Bob was a little baby he had the singular habit of putting his hand under his chin and gazing dreamily into space—a habit, I may add, which his father had. When Mrs. Leslie saw that picture she felt sure that it must be her own dear child, over whose loss she had grieved for nearly fourteen years. Within an hour she made hasty inquiries. She learned enough to make her feel sure. Together we visited Pioneer Street, only to learn that Mr. and Mrs. Tom Temple had kidnaped the boy again. We got the next train, we hurried to Dubuque, we kept the lines busy, and, after the most strenuous day in all my legal career, we landed our little heir in the home of Mose."

"Well," said Anita, "Bob said this is a perfect day. I heard him, and it is."

"Here they come," said Tom Reade.

Masculine cheers and feminine screams greeted the happiest boy in the United States and the sweet-faced woman in black, from whose features had gone forever the sadness and the longing of a mother bewailing her lost child.

"We have had a happy hour," said the

happy mother. "Bob has told me of all his friends. He has told me enough to assure me of what I already had surmised, that God had watched over him through the dearest friends a boy could have. No matter how long I live, my heart, I trust, will ever carry a sense of gratitude to all who have so nobly befriended my boy."

"And," added Bob, giving his mother a glance of love and pride, "it's all fixed. Mother and I are going to travel and get acquainted. And she's going to live up here in Iowa. And next year, Tom and Matt, I'm going to "

Bob paused and smiled.

"To Campion College?" cried both boys breathlessly.

And Bob's answer was drowned in a chorus of voices singing triumphantly:

Campion will shine to-night, Campion will shine, Campion will shine to-night, Campion will shine, Campion will shine to-night, Campion will shine, When the sun goes down And the moon goes up Campion will shine.

THE END

Manufactured by Amazon.ca
Bolton, ON